How do you g

After two hours, my head is spinning
may lose my mind. People seem to feel entitled to ask for
extras, like choice of paper and colour of ribbon and even
the style of the bow! ... Just when I think I may beat the
next person in line to death with their gift, my mom and
Pam show up to cover our break ...

Allison and I make our way over to the food court ...
We slurp our soup as shoppers stream around us like
schools of fish.

"Hey, did you see that elf?" I ask.

"Who, Simon?"

"No, the other one. The one who loads the kids onto
Santa's lap."

"No. Why?" She sips her water.

"I dunno, I think he's pretty cute."

"You mean cute in an elfin way or real-life cute?"

"Real-life cute."

"How are you finding time to wrap gifts *and* check out
elves?"

"Have you seen my gifts?"

Allison laughs. "Yeah. I didn't want to say anything but
your gift-wrapping is pretty awful."

Double-Dare Clare

Raincoast Books gratefully acknowledges the financial support of the Province of British Columbia through the BC Arts Council and the Book Publishing Tax Credit and the Government of Canada through the Canada Council for the Arts and the Book Publishing Industry Development Program (BPIDP).

Edited by Elizabeth McLean
Editorial contributions by Tonya Martin / Joanna Karaplis
Copyedited by Jennifer Charlton
Proofread by Renate Preuss
Cover and interior design by Five Seventeen
Illustrations by Terry Wong

LIBRARY AND ARCHIVES CANADA CATALOGUING IN PUBLICATION

Prinz, Yvonne

Double-dare Clare / Yvonne Prinz.

ISBN 13: 978-1-55192-983-5
ISBN 10: 1-55192-983-X

I. Title.

PS8631.R56D68 2008   JC813'.6   C2008-900354-3

Library of Congress Control Number: 2008920500

Raincoast Books	*In the United States:*
9050 Shaughnessy Street	Publishers Group West
Vancouver, British Columbia	1700 Fourth Street
Canada V6P 6E5	Berkeley, California
www.raincoast.com	94710

Raincoast Books is committed to protecting the environment and to the responsible use of natural resources. We are working with suppliers and printers to phase out our use of paper produced from ancient forests. This book is printed with vegetable-based inks on 100% ancient-forest-free, 100% post-consumer recycled, processed chlorine- and acid-free paper. For further information, visit our website at www.raincoast.com/publishing/.

Printed in Canada by Marquis

10   9   8   7   6   5   4   3   2   1

Double-Dare Clare

BOOK THREE IN
THE CLARE SERIES
BY

Yvonne Prinz

RAINCOAST BOOKS

Vancouver

This book is dedicated to
the Rainforest Action Network, www.ran.org.
Get involved now and help clean up our planet!

Acknowledgements

Merci: BFF Alex Green, Lori Katz, Karen Masterson, Margaret Crowe, Gail Wadsorth, Ladies Of The Chorus; Raincoasters: Jesse Finkelstein, Tonya Martin, Joanna Karaplis; my agent, Sarah Cooper; Elizabeth McLean, Andrew Williamson for daily affirmations, and Dave for the space.

Chapter 1

CHRISTMAS SUCKS! is written in uneven, jagged black letters above the manger scene. Someone spray-painted it right over the curly gold Latin writing on the wooden scroll that says, STABLE FOR RENT — CHEAP. Or at least that's what I always assumed it said. Below the vandalized sign, inside the mini-stable, the life-size statues of Mary, Joseph, the three wisemen (bearing their various shiny gifts), a donkey, a cow and a couple of angels seem untouched. Mary and Joseph, who are positioned on either side of the official "Bed of Straw," anxiously await the arrival of the Baby Jesus any day now. They look a little road weary — more from being dragged out of the school storage room year after year than from trying to find Bethlehem with no compass, no map and no road signs, just a star of wonder and light. Technically, the manger isn't quite empty because right now there are two discarded beer cans nestled in the straw right where the Baby Jesus goes.

Our school used to be called St. Boniface and it was a Catholic school filled with Catholic kids, but somewhere along the way, someone noticed that white Catholic kids were being outnumbered by kids of various religions and colours so they scrapped the whole Catholic school idea and renamed our school Brian Lee Thompson Junior High, after a fireman who fished

an entire drowning family out of the river a few years
back. There's a big picture of him in the front lobby of
the school grinning in his navy fireman's uniform as
the mayor hands him an important award of some sort.
Needless to say, it took the kids a nanosecond to shorten
Brian Lee Thompson to BLT and now I go to a school
named after a delicious toasted sandwich.

The manger scene is a leftover from the St. Boniface
days, but inside the school there's a giant menorah for
Hanukkah and a festive Kwanza display with a kinara and
a bounty of fruits and vegetables.

Just to make sure no one's left out, one week out of
each month of the school year is devoted to a different
ethnic cuisine, which, during Middle Eastern week,
prompted the well-known phrase, "I ate a falafel and now
I feel awful!"

Allison and I crunch through the snow in our boots
and join the small crowd of students gathered in front
of the main entrance. Principal Davidson, red-faced and
jacketless, hurries out of the big double doors with our
school custodian, Eddie, at his heels. Principal Davidson
waves his arms in all directions, ordering Eddie to remove
the vandalized sign and the beer cans before anyone else
sees them, but judging by the gathered crowd, I think he
might be a little late.

Unfortunately, Eddie isn't particularly tall and he has
to jump to reach the sign. He whacks at it like it's a piñata
at a birthday party and after a few tries, the wooden scroll

comes crashing down onto the donkey's head, knocking its left ear clean off. Thankfully, Eddie jumps out of the way in time, but sends Mary face first into the manger. Allison and I cannot look at each other for fear of collapsing into giggles. Poor Eddie stands Mary upright again and brushes the straw off her face and shoulders. He gathers up the fibreglass donkey, the sign and the severed ear and tries to wrangle them through the double doors. Principal Davidson follows behind with the empty beer cans, holding them as far away from his body as possible, as though they might contain plutonium. Eddie has trouble negotiating the doors and the donkey gets stuck half in, half out until Principal Davidson comes from behind and gives it a shove, propelling Eddie and his various parts down the school hallway. Out of the corner of my eye, I can see Allison's shoulders shaking and then I hear her quietly snorting, trying to suppress laughter. I still can't meet her eyes.

Suddenly, Principal Davidson turns back to face the crowd. His ugly Christmas-themed tie flaps up in the wind and smacks him in the face. He quickly yanks it out of the way. "Don't you people have classes to get to?" he shouts angrily, each word making a little white puff in the chilly air.

We disperse and head into the school. The hallways start to buzz with the sound of crime scene talk. Allison and I wander toward our lockers, still snickering. We're feeling very important because we're members of the select group of first-hand witnesses. Sure, it was dumb luck, but we were there. We saw everything.

We reach Allison's locker first and I hold her backpack while she opens her combination lock.

"Well, it does sort of suck," says Allison, wiping tears of laughter from her eyes.

"What?"

"Christmas. It sort of sucks." She takes her backpack from me and unbuckles it, taking out a couple of books. She flings the pack into the bottom of her locker.

I pause, trying to figure out if she's serious. She looks serious. Has she lost her mind? "Well, sure, except for the presents, chocolate, candy, time off from school. Except for that stuff, right?"

Allison continues as though I've said nothing. "It's such a stressful holiday. People run around shopping like maniacs, spending money they don't have, only to have someone return their gift to the store. Christmas is supposed to be about kindness and charity and sharing but it's become something ugly. It's all about mass consumerism."

"Sure, Charlie Brown, but what about the presents and the candy and the chocolate and time off from school?" I ask again.

We're interrupted by Ginny Germain, the most popular girl in our school, who never fails to make an entrance. She's wearing pink sheepskin boots and a matching vest. Amazingly, even her lip gloss matches her outfit. Her locker is right next to Allison's.

"Hey, girls," she says, without even looking at us. "What's everyone got planned for the holidays?" Which means, "How about I tell you what I've got planned for my holiday?"

"Clare and I are volunteering at the gift-wrap booth at the mall."

Ginny stops unlocking her locker and looks at us for the first time. "Seriously?"

We both nod.

"I'm going skiing in Switzerland! Isn't that fabulous?" The fluorescent lights dance off her dazzling white teeth.

"Fabulous," says Allison. She slams her locker door and locks it. We start toward my locker, farther down the hallway. Behind us we can hear Ginny repeating to unsuspecting passersby: "I'm going skiing in Switzerland! Isn't that fabulous?" We look at each other and roll our eyes.

"I used to have a Barbie doll with a tan who said that when you pulled her string. She also said, *Let's go to the beach!* and *Let's put on a fashion show!*"

"Until you pulled her head off," says Allison.

"Right. Until I pulled her head off." Allison knows all my stuff. I sometimes forget. "Actually, she still wants to go to the beach but now she's just a talking torso."

Allison looks back over her shoulder at Ginny as though she might be picturing her as a talking torso.

"Someone should probably warn the Swiss," she says.

We stop at my locker and now Allison holds my pack while I work the combination.

"So, let's get back to your views on Christmas, Mr. Scrooge."

"Yeah, we don't do the big Christmas thing at my house."

"Whaddya mean?"

"My mom's Jewish and my dad's not into organized religion and neither of them likes the whole commercial Christmas thing, so we don't do it."

"So, no tree, no candy canes, no Santa, no gifts?" I ask, startled.

"Well, we exchange gifts but we have to make them."

"What, like macramé plant hangers?"

"Like anything. My dad made me a captain's bed one year and a rocking chair once, too."

"Wow. My dad lives in fear of the words 'assembly required.'"

"... and my mom knitted me an afghan one year."

"Nice," I say, thinking about my family's new version of Christmas; the Christmas where my mom isn't a lawyer anymore. Back when she was a lawyer, Christmas was a bit slapdash. Mom or Dad would hit the tree lot on Christmas Eve and buy the last sad tree, which lost most of its remaining needles on the ride home. They'd set a land-speed record setting it up and then I usually found my mom on Christmas morning slumped over the gifts she was trying to wrap — gifts that had been purchased by her assistant, Doria. One year there was a mix up with the gifts and I got a crystal decanter and a mahogany shoehorn. Before I started school, I think it annoyed my

parents that the daycare I went to closed for the holidays.
They used to try to downplay the whole thing and tell me
that it wasn't the big holiday those "kooky" daycare work-
ers were making it out to be. I knew they were lying,
though. I watched way too much television to let them
get away with that.

Now it's all different. Now my mom's a Christmas nut-
ball, decking the halls, whipping up the eggnog, lighting
the yule log, spreading holiday cheer. She's even the head
of this year's fundraiser for the Breast Cancer Foundation,
a gift-wrapping booth in the mall where Allison and I
will be volunteers (a.k.a. Gift-Wrap Slaves) for the pre-
holiday shopping frenzy.

This is also my first Christmas without Elsa, who's been
living in Paris since last June when I decided that thirteen
was too old to have an imaginary friend. (She hates the
term "Imaginary Friend"; she prefers "Stylist," "Psychic,"
"Life Coach" or "Confidante.") I wanted to go cold turkey
and send her away forever but we eventually settled on
Paris — sort of an imaginary friend relocation program.
Now I'm really glad that she's still out there somewhere:
I wasn't counting on my life taking some of the sharp
right turns it has lately and she's come in pretty handy.
Elsa's also the one who got me through all those bumpy
Christmases from ages four to twelve. She's not really
your average imaginary friend. She's got a lot of attitude.
In fact, there used to be days when I felt like taking out a
restraining order against her. Overall, though, she saved
my life big time. I guess I haven't been the best about

writing her lately. Perhaps I'll send her a *Joyeux Nöel* card tonight. I wonder what her holiday plans are?

Principal Davidson's voice booms over the loudspeaker, interrupting my thoughts. He calls for all students and teachers to attend an assembly in the gymnasium at 9:00 a.m. sharp.

"Hmmm, I wonder what that's all about?" I smirk.

"Most definitely manger-related," says Allison.

Just then Eric, my Drama teacher and the director of the first play I ever acted in, walks by.

"Hey, Clare, what happened out there? I heard the manger got tagged," he says, turning around and walking backwards away from us.

I nod. "It was terrible. A donkey lost an ear."

Eric covers his mouth and his eyes widen in fake horror. "Not the donkey! We love the donkey!"

Allison and I nod simultaneously and look fake-sad.

Eric disappears down the hallway, laughing. We love Eric. He's more like a student than a teacher, and if it weren't for his encouragement, I'd never have auditioned for the part of Lady Macbeth in the school play a couple of months ago. I got the part and I loved it and now I want to be an actress. It really is that simple. At thirteen years old I know exactly what I want to do with the rest of my life.

Allison and I head down to the gymnasium. We find an opening on the polished wood floor and sit down with all the other students to watch Principal Davidson try to sniff out the perp. I don't like his chances. The vandal might not even go to our school. I wonder if he's considered that. The gym fills up around us. Principal Davidson is standing at the podium onstage. He's still red-faced. He clears his throat several times into the microphone and it looks like he's gearing up for a big fat lecture about respect and how we're "young adults and it's time we started behaving like it." That's pretty much his standard speech. Sometimes he likes to mix it up with a few tag lines he picks up from the motivational child psychology books he has stacked in his office. My personal favourite is "Someday is not a day of the week!"

Someone near us yells, "How's the donkey?"

The entire gymnasium erupts into laughter. The teachers standing along the walls of the gym shuffle their feet and look uncomfortable. I'm pretty sure they'd like to be laughing along with everyone else.

"Who said that?" Principal Davidson scours the crowd. No one says a word. "You think this is funny? Well, you might not think this is so funny when I make you all sit here until someone confesses. If you want to behave like children, then you'll be treated like children."

After fifteen minutes of silence (a.k.a. note-passing, face-making, whispering, snickering and armpit farts), Principal Davidson, the king of idle threats, dismisses us, but vows that this is not the end of it. We all shuffle off to our homerooms. The excitement is over for now.

It's three days before school is out for Christmas vacation.

Chapter 2

Elsie, my dog (not to be confused with Elsa in Paris — I know, it's a bit confusing), attacks me at the front door of my house with her standard greeting, which involves knocking people to the floor unconscious and then jumping on top of their lifeless body and licking their face. She's a nine-month-old golden Labrador (a thirteenth-birthday gift from my Aunt Rusty, who, like Elsie, has no boundaries). Elsie is a recent graduate of the Oberdean Obedience School for Puppies, but if puppy school were real school, Elsie would have spent the whole time in the principal's office. During a round of sit-stays, Elsie left the ring entirely and returned with someone's sweater in her mouth. She tried to get me to play tug-of-war with her and she was really hurt when I wouldn't. The owner of the sweater wasn't too happy either. I also thought it was a bad sign that Elsie ate her diploma on graduation day.

"Down, Elsie!" I try to sound firm. Somehow she thinks "down" means "more." Where did I go wrong?

Elsie's frantically wagging tail knocks a delicate, hand-blown, one-of-a-kind Christmas ornament from the pine bough festooning the oak banister. Elsie and I watch as it becomes airborne for a split second and then lands on the oriental carpet with a soft thud, narrowly missing the wood floor where it would have smashed to smithereens. Elsie pounces on it. I pounce on Elsie.

"No, no, NO!" I gently pry open her jaws like the Crocodile Hunter and snatch the glass ball from her mouth. I hang it back on the bough, out of reach, dog spit and all. My mom would flip if she saw what just happened.

As I kick off my boots, I notice a large red bow with a bell hanging off it tied around Elsie's neck.

"Mom!" I yell, "we've talked about this! Please stop decorating the dog!"

My mom replies from the living room, "Oh, honey, it's Christmas! Lighten up!"

I hear her new friend Pam snickering.

I don't have to go in there to know that they're having another one of their "meetings."

Mom and Pam claim to be the steering committee for the gift-wrapping booth at the mall, but the truth is that it took all of fifteen minutes to organize: get wrapping paper, tape, a table, a sign, a jar for donations, and find slave labour (that's where Allison and I come in), and you're done. The rest of the time they spend drinking white wine, lunching and laughing a lot while we're down at the mall doing the actual work. Well actually, we don't start till Saturday when school's out for Christmas and shopping has reached a heightened frenzy.

I suppose I can't complain too much. I'm really happy that my mom found a friend. Before Pam came along I was the friend, and boy did that get old fast. At least Pam can order something stronger than a Shirley Temple in a restaurant, and I'll bet she's more fun to shop with, too. She probably doesn't get her clothes in the junior department. My mom and Pam met at a 5K mother-daughter run for the Breast Cancer Foundation. I was the daughter in that scenario but my mom dumped me pretty fast when she met Pam, possibly the only other person on the planet who actually stopped practising law. Now they sit around telling lawyer jokes.

Pam brings with her a whole posse of friends who don't have much use for the corporate world — in other words, my dad. Coincidentally, Pam is also married to a corporate lawyer. My dad's not thrilled with the new circle of friends. He says they wear weird jewellery, and I think he's afraid my mom will make him join a drumming circle. He makes it sound like her new friends live in caves.

As I make my way down the hallway to the kitchen, I inhale the Christmas-tree-lot smell coming from an entire forest's worth of pine boughs attached to every available surface and an enormous twinkling tree in the living room. It's like my mom's own personal deforestation project. Once in the kitchen, though, the pine smell is overpowered by the hot-mulled smell. There is always something mulling on the stove: apple cider, wine, glogg. (What *is* glogg, anyway? Some sort of Viking drink?) Funny, I've never actually seen anyone in this house drink a hot-mulled beverage. Even when the stove isn't on, there's a hot-mulled candle burning, lest we forget it's Christmas.

More laughter trickles in from the living room, along with a background of baroque Christmas carols. No Chipmunks' Christmas album for my mom; if it's not composed by a dead guy, she's just not interested.

I grab a gingerbread man off a snowman-shaped platter on the counter and pour myself a glass of milk from the fridge. I toss a dog biscuit to Elsie after she obediently sits for it (the one and only thing she learned at puppy school — forget about the staying part, though) and head upstairs to my room with Elsie at my heels, still chewing her biscuit.

A festive wreath is hanging on my bedroom door, hiding the KEEP OUT sign. I remove it and hang it on the bathroom doorknob. Elsie jumps onto my bed and makes herself comfortable. I sprinkle a little fish food into the glass bowl where Maude, my goldfish, lives. She fish-dances with joy. I settle in next to Elsie on the bed and start a long-overdue letter to Paris.

Dear Elsa,

So, it's been practically forever (almost a month) and I can't believe we haven't discussed Christmas. Are you staying in Paris for the holidays? It must be so beautiful there. Is there snow?

It occurred to me today that this will be our first Christmas apart, which is just so strange. Also, Allison told me today that she's not big on the whole Christmas thing, which shocked me and made me miss you terribly. And that's not the worst of it. She told me that she makes all her gifts by hand, which puts unbelievable pressure on me. I can't exactly give her something I just picked up at the mall when she's spent hours hammering or painting or crocheting or knitting or doing whatever it is she has planned for my gift. Maybe I could buy something that looks handmade and tell her I made it. No, that would be deceitful. Besides, I'm a terrible liar. Sigh.

Even though I wish you were here with me, I hope that you have wonderful people to spend the holidays with, and good food and music and gifts and chocolate, of course.

Starting Saturday I'll be working at the mall, wrapping gifts for charity (yawn), so my Christmas is guaranteed to be fun-filled. The gift-wrap table is conveniently situated right next to the North Pole, so at least I get to ask Santa some questions that have been gnawing at me all these years: are the elves unionized? How does one month of real work a year qualify as a job? Don't you worry about your cholesterol going through the roof with all those cookies? Let me know if there's anything you need to know.

Simon Beckman (you remember Simon) is a part-time elf at the North Pole. He's also the Ghost of Christmas Past in the community theatre production of A Christmas Carol. He doesn't have a moment to spare and if he does he spends it with his girlfriend, Sylvia (sigh).

I'd love it if you could drop by for an eggnog or something. You have to see this place. It looks like a Martha Stewart Living magazine exploded. My mom's more than making up for twelve crappy Christmases.

Your fair,

Clare

P.S. Does Santa even come to Paris?

I put down my pen and give Elsie a scratch on her velvety soft head. Snowflakes have started falling softly outside my window. I get off the bed and stand at the window, watching them fall on the rooftop, the place where I do most of my serious thinking (weather permitting). Across the street, Patience, my new psychotic neighbour, is making snow angels in her front yard. She seems to be going for quantity over quality. Her hot pink snowsuit clashes violently with her carrot-coloured hair. The finished angels look like a crooked row of paper dolls.

The sun is disappearing quickly; it seems to fall out of the sky and it gets dark so early now. The snow is awfully pretty though, especially when it's all fresh and powdery. Patience stands with her hands on her hips and surveys her work. She appears satisfied and heads inside. Her mittens are too slippery to work the doorknob on her front door so she starts pounding on it with her little fists until her mom opens it.

As I'm standing there I start to ponder the whole idea of making gifts for Christmas. Maybe Allison and her family are onto something. A homemade gift really is more meaningful. Why couldn't I make gifts for everyone this year? I'm creative. I own a hot glue gun. What's to stop me? I try to imagine the looks on my parents' faces on Christmas morning as they open their homemade gifts: "You *made* this?"

I jump back on the bed with Elsie and start brainstorming.

Chapter 3

Every eighth-grader at BLT has to meet with the guidance counsellor, Ms. Ganz, at some point during the school year. You're assigned an "appointment" the day you pick up your textbooks and you shove it to the back of your brain (or in my case, under a refrigerator magnet) until the day it arrives. For me, that day is today, the last day of school before Christmas vacation. According to my appointment slip, the purpose of this meeting is to "Assess every student and help them find their individual path to success" (or, in some cases, prison). My appointment is scheduled for first thing in the morning. Not a good time for me.

I have to wonder how Ms. Ganz could possibly consider herself an authority on the "Path to Success." She did, after all, end up a guidance counsellor at BLT. She must have taken a wrong turn in there somewhere, or maybe her particular path just came to a dead end.

I also think that this is going to be the shortest meeting ever because, as I mentioned before, I know exactly what I want to do with my life.

Ms. Ganz yells, "It's open!" when I knock. The first thing I see when I enter her cramped office is her ultra-hip, denim-covered rear-end as she digs through her filing cabinet. Her jewellery makes a jangly sound whenever she moves. I wonder why noisy jewellery doesn't get to the person wearing it. Plus, do you always want people to hear you coming? It completely rules out sneaking up on anyone. I stand there, feeling claustrophobic.

"I'll be right with you, Clare. I'm just locating your file."

My file? I have a file? I'm picturing mug shots, fingerprints, lie detector test results and priors. How can there be a file already? This is the first time we've met.

Ms. Ganz appears, file in hand, and comes out from behind the desk. She arranges her face into an interested and supportive expression and adjusts her glasses. She's wearing leopard-skin frames. I picture her going into the optical shop at the mall and saying, "Where do you keep the frames that will make kids think I'm cool?"

"Let's sit down," she says, backing into a flowery upholstered chair (definitely not school-issue). I sit in its twin that's meant to be across from hers, but the office is so small that our knees are almost touching. Ms. Ganz must have learned at guidance counsellor school that it's important to remove all barriers between yourself and the student. I'm thinking, *What I could really use right now is a barrier.* A fussy little crystal bowl of candy canes is gathering dust on a tiny table between the chairs. There isn't a student on earth who would eat one of those things. If you take one, it's like saying, "It's okay for you to tell me what to do with my life even though you don't know the first thing about me."

Ms. Ganz peruses my file. As I fidget in the flowered chair, my eyes drift over to a heart-shaped frame sitting on the desk. Inside the frame is a picture of a big orange cat. The frame is upholstered in the same fabric as my chair and I smell a weekend do-it-yourself project — the kind that sad, single women do as their cats watch, bored out of their minds. Maybe I'm wrong though, maybe there is a Mr. Ganz, or maybe there was a Mr. Ganz. Either way, the cat's more important right now.

I can hear kids whooping and hollering in the hallway.

"So, Clare. It says here that both your parents are law-yers." She looks up at me and remembers to smile.

"I think that file needs to be updated. My mom quit."

"She ... quit?" Ms. Ganz blinks several times.

"Yeah. She quit." I look down and brush imaginary lint off my corduroys.

"Okay." She makes a note in the file and continues undeterred, "And does a career as a lawyer appeal to you, Clare?"

"No," I say with confidence because this is not some-thing I have to think about.

"Well now, let's not be hasty."

I'm starting to wonder if her list of suggested career options reads:

    1. Doctor,

    2. Lawyer,

    3. Indian Chief.

"I want to be an actress," I say, straightening up in my chair and thrusting my chin out a bit just the way I imag-ine an actress might.

"An actress." Again, she blinks repeatedly.

Ms. Ganz looks down at my file again. Her lips move as she reads. "Oh yes, it says here that you played Lady Macbeth in the school's fall production. You must have been adorable. Do you know that I dreamed of being an actress when I was about your age? I actually played Stella in *A Streetcar Named Desire*."

"Really?" I ask. I wonder when her dream veered off into a nightmare and landed her here.

"Clare, I think it's great that you want to become an actress but you have to be practical, too. Are you planning on going to college?"

I shrug. The truth is I haven't given it much thought. My parents may have mentioned a college fund in passing, but for all I know, they may have spent it on a trip to Cabo San Lucas by now. Besides, I'm *thirteen* years old! Ms. Ganz reads my mind.

"Clare, I know that thirteen seems a bit young to start planning all the way down the road to college, but schools are very competitive these days and if you start focusing on what you'd like to do with your future, your chances of becoming a success are so much greater." She shuffles through my file.

I watch some students outside the window. They're having an old-fashioned snowball fight. Some of them are hiding behind a snow-covered bench and another group is standing right in front of Ms. Ganz's tiny window. I recognize a couple of them from the class I'm supposed to be in right now and I wonder why they're not in it. Has war been declared on school while I've been stuck here discussing my future with Ms. Ganz?

"I'm looking at your personality profile here and …"

"What's that?"

"You don't remember filling out a personality profile in September?"

I think back. September was a very busy time for me. I temporarily lost my best friend, Allison, to the diabolical Ginny Germain and things got very complicated. I vaguely remember filling out some sort of FBI-style questionnaire but I sure don't remember giving it much thought.

"Well, your personality profile indicates that your strength lies in public service, like for instance, health care, human relations or social services, things of that nature." I try to imagine the specific question that would reveal that about somebody: *If you saw someone bleeding to death on the side of the road, would you help him or would you keep walking?*

It makes me think of that scene in *Blade Runner* where the replicant is being interviewed by the cop to see if he's a replicant. The cop says, "If you were in the desert and you saw a turtle on its back, would you flip it over?" The replicant says, "What kind of turtle is it?" Then the replicant kills the cop.

Ms. Ganz clears her throat nervously, as though she truly understands the lameness of what she just said.

Part of me feels badly for Ms. Ganz. She must come up against this a lot and maybe she's even good at her job. Maybe some students come in without any direction at all and leave with an eye to a solid future as the office manager in the human resources department of a local manufacturing plant. I just think she should recognize determination when she sees it. I think she should look at students like me and appreciate that we already know where we're going, so her work is done; she gets a free pass to get a coffee or take an early lunch.

I take a deep breath and exhale slowly. Ms. Ganz watches me. I smile thinly.

"I would like to become an actress." I wonder if Meryl Streep had to deal with this.

A snowball splats against the window. Ms. Ganz flinches but says nothing. It makes me think that Ms. Ganz's window is often used for target practice.

"Okay. Let's do it this way. How about a second choice? What would you be if you couldn't become an actress?"

"I don't have a second choice." I look directly into her eyes.

"Well, let's talk about your other skills."

"I don't have any other skills." I cross my arms in front of my chest. This isn't entirely true: I'm a pretty good long-distance runner, but I can't imagine what sort of career that would prepare me for. Bank robber is the only one that comes to mind. I'm also absolutely the best at reciting lines from movies, especially Woody Allen movies. I think this is probably a useless skill (except for an actress).

"Oh, come on." Ms. Ganz tries to sound chummy. "It says here that your math skills are above average and your reading skills are excellent."

Which means what, exactly? That when I grow up I will be able to balance a cheque book and read the manual that comes with my microwave?

I stare at her like I don't speak English. I think this is what's known as a standoff.

She sighs. "Okay, Clare, I'll get some brochures together for acting programs and you can pick them up at the end of the day. Promise me that you'll at least think about college. There are a lot of them out there with excellent drama programs." I can see her keeping score in her head: one more aimless drain on society, one less corporate cog in the wheel.

"Sure. Thank you." I smile for real now. I stand up and awkwardly squeeze past her, trying not to bonk knees with her. I open the office door to pre-Christmas chaos in the hallway. A kid runs by the door holding plastic mistletoe.

I close the door behind me and make my way to class. I feel like I've won a small battle. I stood up to the woman who would have talked me into law school if she could and that's the last thing on Earth I want to do with my life. I'm sure my dad would be thrilled if I used the word "lawyer" in regards to a career choice but my mom would have a stroke.

Chapter 4

Betty presses a long red fingernail onto the gold ribbon, holding it taut, and expertly ties a bow. Tiny purple Christmas lights bob from her earlobes and Rudolph's red nose on her Christmas sweater flickers on and off. Her lips are pursed in concentration.

Allison and I are not wearing festive wear. We don't actually own any. We think that it should be outlawed.

"You see," chirps Betty, clipping the ribbon with scissors, "just make sure you don't use too much ribbon. There you are, sir. I hope your wife enjoys that."

She passes a wrapped Dustbuster to the man at the front of the line. He drops a five-dollar bill into our collection jar. I wonder exactly how one enjoys a Dustbuster, a little machine that picks lint and Cheerios up off the floor. What's to enjoy? Maybe we should also offer a service where we advise people on suitable gifts. For five dollars we'll guarantee that your family will still be speaking to you after they open their gifts.

"Okay," says Betty, "now you try."

Allison jumps in and takes the next person in line, a man holding a train set. She rips the perfect amount of paper off the roll and folds the edges in like a pro. I'm very impressed. I assume she must have developed this talent from years of craft projects and making her own

Christmas gifts (how did I miss the boat on all that?). She works with blinding speed. If there were a gift-wrapping Olympics, all my money would be on Allison.

The man takes the wrapped gift and drops a dollar in the jar.

Allison says curtly, "Thank you, sir, and all the proceeds go directly to finding a cure for breast cancer."

The man looks sheepish and digs a couple more dollars out of his wallet. He tosses them in the jar and walks away quickly. Allison leans out after him and calls cheerfully, "Merry Christmas, sir!"

Betty steps in. "Girls, a donation is voluntary. You mustn't harass the customers." Betty has no idea who she's dealing with. Allison takes these kinds of things very seriously. She told me that when she was in sixth grade, she sold enough chocolate bars door-to-door to outfit her entire school band with uniforms. She outsold the other kids ten-to-one. The weird part is, she wasn't even *in* the band.

I'm up next. I figure I should be great at this since Ms. Ganz cheerfully informed me yesterday that I am "well-suited" for public service. The victim is a pair of fluffy pink slippers for a little girl's grandmother. I rip off way too much paper, use way too much tape and blow the whole ribbon thing. Betty's forehead creases. The little girl looks at me like I just ruined Christmas.

After that, Allison and I work in tandem, taking two customers at a time. When Betty finally feels that I've sort of got the hang of it, she reluctantly leaves us alone. With Betty out of the way, Allison and I set to work with abandon. It soon becomes clear that Allison can take two customers to my one. Her packages also look very tidy whereas mine seem to sport a more "casual" look.

Every time I look up, my eyes drift over to the North Pole next door. Simon, the cashier elf, is in charge of extorting as much money as possible from the mommies for Santa photos. He looks adorable in his green-and-red elf outfit with matching hat and tights and curly-toed shoes that have bells on them. Every now and then he catches my eye and winks at me. I'm a bit envious: at least his job requires some acting, and he gets paid. Unfortunately, you have to be at least fourteen to be an elf. Farther into the winter wonderland, another elf is in charge of arranging how the children will sit on Santa's lap. Even from here I can tell that he hates his job and although he's a victim of unfortunate elf-wear, I can also tell that he's pretty cute. I keep trying to get a better look but the gift-wrap line is endless and since my gift-wrap shortcomings have recently been exposed I have to stay focused. Christmas music is blaring non-stop from the speakers near us and there's a lot of *Ho Ho Hos* and bells jingling next door, not to mention the screaming children.

After two hours, my head is spinning and I feel like I may lose my mind. People seem to feel entitled to ask for extras, like choice of paper and colour of ribbon and even the style of the bow! Allison is doing a magnificent job of keeping her cool, although she continues to strong-arm people into more generous "donations." She uses terms like "life-threatening" and "important research." Just when I think I may beat the next person in line to death with their gift, my mom and Pam show up to cover our break. I could kiss them.

Allison and I make our way over to the food court and quickly narrow down the options. Allison is a vegetarian and I prefer my food edible so we settle on a soup and salad bar. We both get "homemade" vegetable soup and grab a tiny table. We slurp our soup as shoppers stream around us like schools of fish.

"Wow. The energy in here is intense," says Allison, wiping her mouth with a napkin and looking around.

"I know. I think I'm developing a migraine and my index fingers are raw. And by the way, you have tape in your hair."

Allison pulls at her ponytail until she locates the tape and carefully removes it. "I hope we never have to get real jobs like this. I don't think I'm cut out for a retail environment."

We watch in a daze as the woman next to us piles her baby stroller higher than Santa's sleigh and then walks away without her baby, who's happily painting the table with ice cream. She suddenly realizes that she's forgotten something and turns back. Allison and I grin at each other.

"Hey, did you see that elf?" I ask.

"Who, Simon?"

"No, the other one. The one who loads the kids onto Santa's lap."

"No. Why?" She sips her water.

"I dunno, I think he's pretty cute."

"You mean cute in an elfin way or real-life cute?"

"Real-life cute."

"How are you finding time to wrap gifts *and* check out elves?"

"Have you seen my gifts?"

Allison laughs. "Yeah. I didn't want to say anything but your gift-wrapping is pretty awful."

"Thanks. Luckily I only have to do this for seven hundred more hours."

"Well, why don't you ask Simon about him? I'm sure he knows the guy."

"Who?"

"The cute elf. I'm sure Simon knows him, they work together."

Allison is usually the voice of reason, but what she fails to understand is that I could never ask Simon about the elf. Not in a million years. Simon and I kissed once, back when we were in *Macbeth* together. It was just a kiss and it was mostly because he felt sorry for me, but on the off-chance that he ever wanted me to run off with him, I could hardly say, "Well, sure. But only if the thing with the cute elf doesn't work out." Because, as it happens, Simon is perfect. Just ask his perfect girlfriend, Sylvia.

We throw our trash into the overflowing garbage can and head back to our prison cell. On the way, we stop at the window of a jewellery store and look at gold watches.

"Okay, if you had to buy one, which would it be?" I ask.

Allison presses her nose against the glass. "Hmmm, they're all SO ugly. Which one could I bear? Would I have to wear it or could I sell it?"

"You have to wear it," I say. "Every day."

While Allison is choosing, I look through the glass at the woman ringing up a customer's jewellery purchase. She looks awfully familiar but I can't quite place her. She's wearing a coral-coloured cashmere sweater and her greyish-brown hair is cut short and neat. A pair of lavender reading glasses hangs around her neck on a delicate chain. It suddenly dawns on me that it's Paul's mom. Paul was my only friend in the world (until I met Allison), and he left to attend a private boys' school clear across the country last July because his mom checked into a rehab centre for alcoholics. Well, also because his dad, who's a total weirdo, is obsessed with his education. Paul's parents are a lot older than mine. They're also divorced. I walk inside the store for a better look.

"Hey. Where ya goin'?" asks Allison.

"Be right back. Keep shopping."

As I get closer, Paul's mom recognizes me. Her mouth turns up into a slow smile, something I don't think I've seen her do before. She looks beautiful.

"Clare? Is that you, honey?"

"Hi, Mrs. Bennett. I didn't know you worked here."

"Oh, I just started a couple of months ago. It's only part-time."

"How's Paul?"

"Well, you can ask him yourself. He'll be coming home later tonight for the holidays."

How could I not have remembered that Paul would be home for the holidays? How could I possibly have let so much time pass without even thinking about him once? Am I really that selfish? The last time I saw him, I was standing in his driveway in the rain weeping as his mom's car disappeared around the corner. What happened after that? Apparently I'd carried on with my life.

"Will he call me when he gets in?" I ask.

"I'm sure he'll do more than that. Weren't you two the best of friends?" She smiles again.

"Yeah, I guess we were." I pause for a second. "Mrs. Bennett, you look really great."

She looks down and I know she must be thinking about what she used to look like or what she used to be like. But there's not a trace of that left. The old Mrs. Bennett, who walked around in caftans and dark glasses, carrying a martini in the middle of the day, is long gone.

"Thank you, Clare," she says quietly.

I tell her about the gift-wrapping booth and she says she's sure we'll bump into each other again soon.

"Who was that?" asks Allison as I join her in front of the store.

"That's Paul's mom."

"Who's Paul?"

"A friend. You'll meet him soon."

As we head back through the mall, I see the cute elf approaching from the other direction. He's carrying his elf hat in his hand and his hair is sticking out in all directions. His big blue eyes are not the eyes of a jolly elf. They're the eyes of someone who wants out of the North Pole altogether. I nudge Allison and we watch him walk past us. Allison sucks in her breath.

"Wow, you were right about the cute part, but he looks like he got kicked by a reindeer."

I look over my shoulder and watch him disappear into the crowd of shoppers.

Chapter 5

I open my front door and there stands Paul, just as if he'd never left. I'm not quite ready for him to be standing there. I'm expecting Allison, who's supposed to drop by with her mom and pick me up for our slave jobs at the mall, but her mom is always running late. I'm also sort of expecting Patience, my insane six-year-old neighbour, who never fails to drop by just as I'm going out the door to show me her gum or her latest artwork or a bug. If no one's home, she shoves it through the mail slot. And then Elsie eats it. I know this because sometimes I'm sitting on the stairs in the dark, pretending not to be home.

After I pull Elsie off of Paul (he's eyeing her like she's a killer grizzly), I invite him inside and get a better look at him. He stands in the front hallway, snow melting off his boots. His cheeks are pink from the cold. He's a bit taller now and his hair doesn't look like he cuts it himself anymore. He's got a touch of acne on his chin but nothing serious. His glasses are new, too, and I have to admit, he looks almost normal.

I try to remember that this is the guy I spent almost all my spare time with until he left last July. And yet, standing here, I don't feel close to him at all. I feel like I could probably jump back in and hang out like we used to, but since I met Allison I realize that friendship is more than just hanging out together. Of course, once we start talking, I realize that Paul will always be Paul: awkward, uncomfortable and famous for saying the wrong thing.

"Well, here I am," he shrugs. "Home for the holidays."

"Yes." I think about hugging him but we've never hugged. Kids my age are doing a lot of excessive hugging these days. They don't see each other for an hour and they hug like one of them was lost at sea for years or something. I tend not to hug.

I repeat myself. "Yes. Here you are." I guess I can't expect to fall into the same conversations we used to have for hours at a time (never anything personal, of course). But aren't we the same people except for some small physical changes, like, for instance, I now have breasts and I'm even taller? It would be just like Paul not to notice these things though.

An awkward moment passes and then I think of something.

"Hey, I'm really sorry that I never wrote you but …" I trail off. "Well, you know how it is."

"Yeah. I sent you that one postcard and then things got sort of busy." He looks at his feet.

"I'd invite you in but I'm sort of on my way out. I'm working at the mall till Christmas."

"Right. My mom told me."

I nod. Another awkward moment passes. "Hey, how's school?"

"Good." Now *he* nods. "Really good."

"Good." Just when I think I may die from the worst conversation ever, the doorbell saves me. It's Allison. I make a big hairy deal of introducing her to Paul.

"Look who it is! It's Allison!" She gives me an odd look. "Allison, this is my friend Paul, the one I was telling you about!"

Paul steps forward and shakes Allison's hand, or not so much her hand as a big fluffy mitten.

"A pleasure to meet you, Allison," says Paul.

"Same here." She smiles and I roll my eyes at her but she's not even looking at me. She's looking at Paul like it actually *is* a pleasure to meet him. How is that possible?

Elsie is in heaven with yet another person to jump on. I tell her to sit, which she does for a nanosecond.

"Clare, we should get going. My mom's waiting in the car and she has to get to her yoga class."

"Sure. Um, Paul, walk us out, okay?"

I grab my coat and pull my boots on. I shove Elsie inside and close the front door behind me. Three seconds later, her face appears in the front window.

Paul leads the way and holds the car door open for Allison. I'm on my own. I jump in the back seat of Allison's mom's old Volvo (her "new" car that burns French fry oil) and say hi to her. I roll down the window and tell Paul that I'll call him later and we'll do something. He seems okay with that.

As we drive up the street, I can see Allison watching him in the side mirror. She turns around in her seat.

"So, you've been holding out on me?"

"Whaddya mean?"

"Paul."

"What about him?"

"He's cute."

"Cute? Seriously? I guess I never really looked at him that way."

"Tell me some more about him."

"Um . . . hmm, well, he's really, really smart — like scary smart. Let's see, what else? He's a great Scrabble player, he loves old Japanese monster movies and he's a mad scientist. He'll probably win the Nobel Prize for inventing a cure for something life-threatening one day . . ."

"He sounds great!"

Allison's mom chuckles.

"Wait, I'm not finished. He's the lamest athlete on the planet. Trees scare him. He can't swim, he's paranoid, he's a germaphobe, he's a very picky eater, he's afraid of animals, he's allergic to everything and he doesn't know girls exist."

"So, you don't think he has a girlfriend?"

I snort. "I think that's a pretty safe bet."

Allison smiles and turns back around in her seat. Her mom looks over at her and smiles too.

I look out the car window at the houses passing by. It's close to four o'clock and the Christmas lights are starting to come on. I think about Paul, and about how Allison and I see him so differently. Could she really be considering him as boyfriend material? How absurd is that? Allison's been asked out by lots of guys at our school and for a while there, this guy named Troy, a handsome jock, was obsessed with her. He finally stopped pursuing her about a month ago, but I think she broke his heart. I wish I could be as selective as Allison, but if I could, I sure wouldn't select Paul.

The mall glimmers like Las Vegas in the distance. As we get closer, traffic is jammed in all directions so Allison and I hop out and snake through the cars and dirty snow on foot, arriving at the gift-wrapping booth just in time. Betty looks like she's nearing a nervous breakdown. A lock of hair is hanging in her eyes and her lipstick is smeared. Also, Rudolph's nose has a dead battery and Betty doesn't seem to care. She's really happy to see us. She quickly grabs her purse and stumbles away in a daze. I glance over at the North Pole. Simon's not working, but the cute grumpy elf is hoisting a chubby baby onto Santa's lap.

A few customers in (and I don't mind saying that my gifts are starting to look much better), I come face-to-face with Ginny Germain, arms full of unwrapped gifts. She's wearing a soft white scarf wrapped loosely around her neck and a powder-blue wool sweater. Her unbearably shiny black hair shimmers on her shoulders.

"Oh, look! It's Clare and Allison. How sweet! Can I get you to be careful with these?" She shoves her stack of gifts at us.

"I thought you were going skiing in Switzerland," says Allison.

"Tomorrow morning, first thing. We're exchanging gifts tonight; it's like I get two Christmases! Hey, do you mind if I just leave these with you? I have some last-minute things to pick up."

She doesn't wait for a response and she's gone with a toss of her hair. When she's out of earshot I respond, "No, of course we don't mind. Do you mind if we wrap these in toilet paper?" Allison snickers and gets to work on Ginny's gifts that include: a crystal bowl, a set of brandy snifters, a cashmere wrap and a pearl brooch.

"Wow," she says. "Who's on her Christmas list? The Queen of England?"

I look over from the book I'm wrapping for the next person in line. Ginny's gifts look a lot like the "corporate gifts" my mom used to give when she was a lawyer — pretty weird gifts for a thirteen-year-old to be giving. I'm suddenly reminded that I have very little time left to make gifts for everyone. So much for that idea. I'll be lucky if I even get Allison's made; in fact, I haven't even thought about what I'm going to make for her. What was I thinking?

Ginny comes back thirty minutes later toting more shopping bags and glowing. We hand her the stack of gifts and she tosses a twenty-dollar bill into our jar like she's tipping a shoeshine boy. It's somehow humiliating.

"Well, I'm off to the Alps. Merry Christmas, you two!" She smiles her best Beauty Queen smile.

"Merry Christmas," says Allison quietly. "Break both legs."

After two hours of non-stop wrapping, I step out the back door of the mall for a breath of fresh air. Allison's gone ahead to get us a place in line at the food court. My mom and Pam are covering for us. So far the ratio of my hours in hell compared to my mom's is four-to-one. All I can say is she had better be planning something fabulous for Christmas.

I sit on the frozen concrete bench and take a deep breath; in with the good fresh air, out with the bad mall air. I start to feel better, even though my lungs are probably freezing. I close my eyes for a moment.

A few seconds later, I hear a soft jingling as someone sits down next to me on the concrete bench. I open my eyes. It's the cute grumpy elf. He looks over at me and grins.

Chapter 6

The cute grumpy elf is looking right into my eyes. Up close, his eyes are an even paler shade of blue. His lips are very red and one front tooth irresistibly overlaps the other. He pulls a cigarette out of a pack and offers me one.

"No, thanks. I um ... don't smoke." This probably isn't the best time to tell him that I took a "No Tobacco Pledge" at school.

He shrugs and lights his cigarette like James Bond, except he uses a cheap plastic lighter instead of a sleek silver one. I think about telling him that smoking stunts your growth but then I remember he's an elf.

"You're the gift-wrap girl," he says, inhaling.

I smile (he knows who I am!). "And you're the elf."

He nods. "Hey, don't tell anyone you saw me smoking, okay? We're not supposed to smoke in costume."

"Sure. I won't." I try desperately to think of a clever comeback to that but I come up empty.

"I saw you talking to Ginny Germain back there. You a friend of hers?"

"No. We go to the same school. BLT."

He raises one eyebrow and looks amused.

"What?" I ask.

"Oh, um, nothing. One of my bandmates goes to your school."

"You're in a band?" It's all I can do not to swoon.

"Uh-huh. I'm a drummer."

"What are you called?"

"Dr. Frankenstein's Easy Chair."

"I don't think I've heard of you. What kind of music is it?"

"We call it Post-Apocalyptic Punk."

I nod. Am I supposed to know what Post-Apocalyptic Punk means? I'm getting in over my head so I change the subject.

"How do you know Ginny?"

"We hung out for a bit last summer. Things were going really great and suddenly the real Ginny showed up and she was all attitude. I told her she should get over herself. I guess she didn't like that very much." He turns his head away from me and exhales smoke in the opposite direction. He turns back. "I'm Vince, by the way."

"I'm Clare."

"Well, nice to meet you, Clare."

"You, too." I look away, suddenly embarrassed. I try desperately to think of something clever to say. What's happened to the clever Clare? Why has she abandoned me? I watch his long thin fingers holding the cigarette. He has the most beautiful hands I've ever seen.

"So, what's it like to work for Santa?" Could that have come out any lamer?

He stomps out his half-smoked cigarette with his pointy-toed elf boot. "I've been peed on, yelled at, slapped, punched and my back hurts from lifting all those fat kids. What do you think it's like working for Santa?"

"So, he's not jolly or anything?"

"There's three of them and none of them are jolly."

"Oh."

Vince stands up. "So, Clare. What's up for Christmas vacation? Any parties?"

The very idea that Vince thinks I might know where the parties are is deeply flattering. Do I actually look like a party girl?

"Um, I don't really know. I've sort of been stuck down here at the mall."

"Hey, I know what you mean. Well, I know about one this weekend. You wanna come?"

I shrug and try to look casual. "Sure."

"Good. Give me your phone number inside and I'll get you the details."

"Okay."

He positions his pointy elf hat on his head.

"Later, Clare," he says, nodding, and heads back inside the mall, the little bells on his hat tinkling as he walks.

I sit there stunned for a few seconds. What just happened? Was I just asked out on a date? Was I just asked out on a date by a drummer in green tights? I give Vince a couple of seconds of lead time and then I jump up and dash inside to tell Allison.

I catch up with Allison at the soup counter, lifting a ladleful of soup and eyeing its contents suspiciously.

"Hey, what took you so long?"

"Sorry. I was just chatting with Vince."

"Who's Vince?"

"The cute grumpy elf."

She fills her bowl with soup and hands me an empty one. "You met the cute grumpy elf? Where?"

"Outside!"

"What was he doing outside?"

"Smoking. But that's not important right now."

"Smoking! Clare, that's disgusting!" She ladles vegetable soup into my bowl. I wanted cream of mushroom but I'm too excited to mention it.

"He asked me to go to a party!"

"With him?"

I think about this for a few seconds. Did he actually ask me to go with him? "Well, he asked me if I wanted to go to a party. I assume he meant with him." I stop at the cooler and grab two sodas.

"A party? Where?" She carries our tray to the checkout. The bored cashier snaps her gum and totals up the tray. We dig out our money.

"I don't know. Why are you all of a sudden consumed with geographical locations?"

"Well, I mean, whose party is it?"

"I dunno." I grab a handful of crackers and two plastic spoons and drop them on our tray.

"Did you say yes?" she asks.

"I think so."

We stand at the edge of the food court, trolling for an empty table in the sea of shoppers. The spaces between the tables are strewn with shopping bags, strollers and children.

"Do you think your mom will let you go?"

"I don't know. She might if you say that you're going."

"You want me to come with you? I don't know, Clare."

"It's not till the weekend. That's almost a week away. You don't have to decide yet."

"Well, we'll see."

Allison spies a just-vacated table and we run for it. She puts the tray down and I carefully pick the trash up off the table using only my pinky fingers and dump it in the nearby garbage can. I sit across from her and pop open my soda.

"Sheesh, Allison, you sound just like my mom."

"Sorry. You're right. I'm glad you met someone new. I'm just looking out for you. Hey, are we still going to Simon's play tomorrow night?"

"Sure, why?"

"Well, I was thinking that we could invite Paul along."

"Okay. I'll call him tonight when I get home. So, we're done talking about Vince?"

Allison smiles and dips her spoon into her soup. "Of course not. Tell me everything."

Later that night, I get into bed, exhausted. I feel as though the mall is sucking the life out of me. At night I have nightmares about enormous piles of gifts that need to be wrapped. Christmas Eve is two days away. I can't wait.

Earlier, I'd slipped my phone number to Vince when he was between customers. I felt horribly self-conscious as I handed it to him and I could feel myself blushing all the way up to my scalp. He didn't seem to notice. I was really glad that I'd resisted the urge to put a smiley face or a heart on the note. He casually took it from me and slipped it into the pocket of his velvet elf pants. It seemed as if getting girls' phone numbers was something he did all day long.

Just before I go to sleep, I scribble a letter to Elsa.

Dear Elsa,

I hope that things are going well for you this Christmas season. As I mentioned, Allison and I are gift-wrapping at the mall. It all sounded so easy when my mom proposed it to me back in November: a few hours here and there and good karma for life. But now I'm thinking about calling the Child Labour Board and asking if it's legal to make kids work this hard. There's got to be about a million laws that my mom is breaking, even if it is for charity.

Just before school let out for the holidays, I had an appointment with the career counsellor, Ms. Ganz, and she told me that I would be suited for public service or human relations. Well, I think this little stint at the mall proves that I couldn't be less suited for public service and I really can't relate to humans at all.

In other news (and I can't believe I saved this for last), I'm going on a date with one of Santa's elves. His name is Vince and I've been watching him for a while now (when I can, what with the rigorous demands of my work) and it turns out he was watching me (ME!), too! He dated Ginny Germain last summer but he broke up with her. I can just picture her face: "YOU'RE breaking up with ME?" Anyway, he plays drums in a band and he's just about the cutest guy I've ever laid eyes on, even in tights. So, I'll keep you posted. Yippee!

Oh, I almost forgot. Paul's back for Christmas and Allison somehow finds him attractive (inconceivable!). We're going to Simon's play tomorrow night, and Allison asked me to ask Paul to come along. I guess if he accepts I'll be the third wheel. I certainly didn't see that coming!

Still the fairest of them all,

Clare

As I'm falling asleep I think about Vince's hands again, the curve of his long fingers on the bench, holding his hat, holding a cigarette. I think about his pale blue eyes and his pink lips and that beautiful crooked front tooth.

Chapter 7

The nights that my mom and dad and I eat dinner at the same time, in the same place, occur about as often as a lunar eclipse. Tonight is one of those rare nights. I've already worked my "mall shift" and later I'm going to see Simon play the Ghost of Christmas Past in *A Christmas Carol*. I called Paul and invited him along. He was delighted. I reminded him that he hates plays and he denied ever saying that so I told him the exact date, time and what we were doing when he said it: last November 21st, 8:00 p.m., about half an hour into *Cats*. He was quiet for a moment and then he said, "It's musicals I hate. I love plays." So Paul's coming.

My mom serves up lasagna and salad in the enchanted pine forest formerly known as the dining room. I move a reindeer candle holder out of the way so I can see my dad. My mom shoots me a look. She doesn't like people messing with her motif. She and my dad are discussing their Christmas schedule. It's not the first time that my mom's new "Free and Easy" circle of friends has collided with my dad's boring, uptight law firm obligations. It's just one of the hazards of "reinventing yourself," which is what my mom is doing and which she likes to mention a lot now that she has a clever name for it (compliments of her new friend Pam).

Elsie sits on the floor at my feet with her nose resting on my knee. In Dog, that means, "Don't forget, I'm here and I'm hungry." Occasionally her paw joins her nose on my knee, which means, "No, really. I'm right here." She throws in the occasional low puppy growl, too, which means, "Yup, still here."

"Let's see ..." says my mom as she passes my dad a plate of lasagna, "I'll leave Pam's party early and come over to the cocktail party at the firm ... hmmm, so I'll have to bring a cocktail dress and change in the ladies' room. Then the next day we'll meet downtown for the partners' dinner, but we'll have to leave early to make it to Tom and Diane's get-together. Of course, I'll have to put the cheese puffs in the trunk but they should be okay. I can just pop them in her oven for a minute."

She's lost my dad. He's taking quick bites of his salad and thinking about something else entirely. He's also watching her wrist move because she's wearing a huge African-looking bracelet. I know that he knows that this bracelet is also compliments of Pam. I'm sure he suspects that a hostile takeover by the "Free and Easys" can't be far off.

"Does that sound good, honey?" My mom takes a sip of wine.

My dad nods and changes the subject. "Clare. I think you might be neglecting your dog. She left me a little surprise on the kitchen floor when I got home today. You haven't forgotten our deal, have you?"

I look down at Elsie. She won't make eye contact.

"Dad, in case you haven't noticed, I've been crazy busy!"

"She's right," my mom chimes in, "but it's only a few more days."

"How's it going down there at the mall, anyway?" asks my dad.

"It's brutal, Dad! You have no idea!"

"I'm sure I don't."

My mom chimes in again, "It's a very nice thing that you're doing, Clare." I suspect she doesn't want me to bring up her actual mall-time versus lunching-with-Pam-time.

"We must have raised a million dollars so far. I feel like I'm curing breast cancer all by myself! One stupid wrapped gift at a time."

Both parents ignore me. "Oh, by the way," says my mom, "your aunt called earlier. She wants to know what you want for Christmas. Can you give her a call? And be very specific. I don't always approve of her interpretation of a gift." She shoots a look at Elsie, my Aunt Rusty's latest gift. My dad looks at the bracelet again.

Suddenly, the doorbell rings. We all freeze and stare at the front door. A couple of seconds later we hear muffled knocking as though the knocker is wearing mittens. We continue watching the front door in silence. The mail slot flies open and a red piece of construction paper with macaroni glued to it is jammed through the opening. Elsie catches it before it even hits the floor. She crunches the macaroni and spits out bits of construction paper. We hear little footsteps growing fainter and then we all brace ourselves for the sound of screeching brakes. Patience has only recently learned to look both ways before crossing the street and that was only after she was hit by a car on Thanksgiving. We all exhale and start eating again.

"I know I should feel guilty," says my mom, "but she's already been over here twice today and one of the times she stayed for an hour telling me about 'Jordan, the guy who spits when he talks.'"

After dinner, as I'm getting ready to leave, I call Aunt Rusty. The phone rings several times and then a guy answers.

"*Haloo?*"

"Um," I pause, confused. "Is Rusty home?"

"*Und* who, may I ask, *ees callink*, please?"

"It's her niece, Clare." (*Und who, may I ask, is answerink my aunt's phone*?!)

"One moment." I hear him, muffled, yell, "Angela! *Eet's* a *leetle* girl; your niece, she says."

Aunt Rusty comes to the phone.

"Hey, Clare, what's up?"

"Who the heck was that?"

"That's Gunther. He's an art dealer from Germany."

"He sounds creepy."

"He doesn't mean to."

"Well, he does. Is he your new boyfriend?"

"Well, he's not delivering pizza."

"Very funny. My mom says you want to know what I want for Christmas."

"Oh, right. That was hours ago. I was calling from the store and when I didn't hear back I just went ahead and bought it so I guess I don't need to know anymore, but trust me, you'll love it."

"Okay. Hey, guess what?"

"What?"

"I sort of met this guy."

"Really, where?"

"At the mall. He's one of Santa's elves."

"I'm intrigued. Continue."

"Well, nothing's happened but he invited me to a party."

I hear Gunther in the background. He sounds angry.

"Sweetie, I gotta run. We're on our way out to a reception. We'll talk some more on Christmas Day, okay?"

"Are you bringing Gunther?"

"Yes, and promise me you'll be nice to him, 'cause your mom's gonna hate him."

"Okay, sure."

"Mwah!" she hangs up the phone.

I throw on my jeans and a green turtleneck. I hear the doorbell downstairs and I know it must be Allison. We're picking Paul up on the way.

Sometimes — like when you spend too much time in a mall — you can forget what Christmas is supposed to be about. It starts to snow softly as Allison and I crunch along in our boots. We look up at the streetlights where flakes swirl around like they do in a snowglobe. Every house on the street features a Christmas tree all lit up in the window, and coloured lights twinkle on porches and fences and roof-tops. This is what Christmas is supposed to feel like.

We stop at Paul's house and I'm surprised to see that it's decorated like all the others on the block; it used to look abandoned. His mom opens the door and welcomes us in. The house is warm and inviting. There's a kind-looking man sitting on the sofa who seems vaguely familiar. Paul's mom introduces him to us as "Bob." He's one of those people who smiles with his eyes as well as his mouth. Paul appears, dressed for an Arctic expedition, and we set out for the community theatre together.

"So, who's that guy on your mom's sofa?" I ask.

"You don't recognize him?"

"He looks familiar," says Allison.

"It's Santa. From the mall."

"Your mom's dating Santa?!" I look back at the house. I guess I'm expecting to see a sleigh and eight tiny reindeer parked out front. All I see is an old station wagon.

"That's so cool," says Allison. "There's no Mrs. Claus?"

"No, she passed away, and for the record, Santa turns back into Bob, the retired insurance adjuster, at midnight on Christmas Eve," Paul says.

Sometimes I forget that Paul's parents are a lot older than mine, especially his dad. Of course, that didn't stop him from moving in with a much younger, pink-spandex-wearing personal trainer named Tamara. I've always been a little creeped out by Paul's dad. As far as I'm concerned, Paul's mom dating Santa is a big step up from Paul's dad.

"It's so great that your mom's dating." Then I add, "Have you seen your dad yet?"

"No. I'm going there on Christmas Eve. Unfortunately, during the holidays, familial obligations are hard to avoid."

"Well, at least your mom won't be alone now that she's dating Santa."

"Bob," Paul corrects me.

As we approach the community theatre, I see Eric, my Drama teacher, coming from the other direction. His curly red hair pokes out from under a super-geeky wool hat. He's holding hands with his wife, who's a nurse. They're about the most adorable couple I've ever seen. He smiles and waves and we all go in together. There's a Christmas tree lit up in the lobby and everyone looks happy. A theatre volunteer hands us a program and we find our seats. Allison has given me strict instructions to make sure she gets to sit next to Paul, so there's a bit of awkward fumbling as we figure out seating without Paul knowing it's all premeditated.

Once I'm settled in and I've removed the first four layers of my clothes, I take a good look around at the small but enthusiastic crowd. Wouldn't it be great if Christmas were just about this? Wouldn't it be great if it were about being happy just because it's snowing and you're at your friend's play?

The lights go down and the curtain goes up. Ebenezer Scrooge sits at a desk in his counting house.

After the play, we all hang around the lobby and wait for Simon to come out from backstage. He was absolutely brilliant as the Ghost of Christmas Past and we all tell him so, even Paul. Simon hugs me, Eric and Allison and gets greyish-green makeup on our cheeks. We put our layers of clothes back on and head out into the cold night.

Paul walks in the middle and chats to Allison about his school and the experiments he's working on. Allison couldn't be more interested and I know she's not faking it. I drift off into my own thoughts, or that is, back to the one thought that's been nagging at me since yesterday: why hasn't Vince called me?

Chapter 8

He called! He called! He called! When I got home from the play last night there was a note stuck to the refrigerator. In my mom's handwriting, it said: *Vince called, 7:30 p.m. Call him back, 432-9900. P.S. Who's Vince?*

I dialled the number immediately. It rang several times and then a woman with a hoarse voice picked up.

"Hello?" Rock music was playing in the background.

"Hi, is Vince home?"

"Hang on," she said, and then I heard her yell, "Hey, turn that down! Is your brother home?"

I waited. She came back after a few seconds.

"No. I don't think he's here. Is this Vicky?"

"No. It's Clare." *Who's Vicky?* "Will you tell him I called, please?"

"Sure hon, I will." But somehow I doubted the message would get to him.

And now I'm at the mall and Vince is over at the North Pole and I don't know if he knows I called him back or not, but my excuse to talk to him just walked off the escalator. Patience has arrived for her annual Santa visit. I've never witnessed it first-hand but I've heard that when Patience leaves the North Pole, it's never quite the same.

I'm glad that I paid special attention to my "look" today. I'm wearing my most flattering baby blue T-shirt with Koko the gorilla on the front layered over a long-sleeved white cotton shirt and my jeans are ripped just perfectly. My hair is clean but I've applied a product that makes it look like I've been to the beach (very authentic in December). The overall effect says "casually bored." Elsa would never approve. Allison, who's wearing a similar outfit (except her T-shirt is tie-dyed), loves it.

Patience is extremely focused on today's mission. She pulls her mother behind her like an eager pup as she zigzags through the holiday shoppers. I can see that she's also paid special attention to her "look" today. She's wearing a stunning holiday ensemble: reindeer antlers, a red-and-green striped pullover with something purple and sticky-looking on the front, a red felt skirt that looks a lot like a Christmas tree skirt (and probably is), candy-cane-striped tights and purple snow boots. The outfit is cleverly pulled together with a furry pink teddy bear backpack. I shudder to think what she's got in there.

Patience and her mom get in line for Santa and I watch them the way you'd watch a car that's about to smash into another. Waiting is not one of Patience's strongest qualities (and the irony of that isn't lost on me). I ask Allison to cover for me and walk over and say hi to Patience and her mom. By the time I get there Patience has already annoyed almost everyone in line.

"Clare!" she says. "You crazy knucklehead! How did you get here?"

"Hi, Patience. I work here."

"Oh. Do you know Santa personally, because this line is really long and if you could talk to him and tell him it's really important that I see him, maybe I could get in faster?"

This gets some half-turns and a few nasty looks from the people in line.

"Um, I'll see what I can do."

I start walking toward the front of the line. When I'm halfway to the front Patience yells, "Tell him I have a very long list to go over!" Her mother covers her mouth.

Simon is cashiering and fortunately he's already met Patience. Well, not so much met her as sat beside her bed with me at the hospital (after she got run over on Thanksgiving), which was also, by the way, the location of our kiss. I walk over to his cash register.

"Simon," I say quietly, "do you think we could get Patience to the front of the line? You know what will happen if she has to wait."

Simon looks at Patience and calls Vince over. Vince walks over and smiles at me and I get positively weak in the knees. I explain the Patience situation, adding a bit of background so he really gets it. Vince eyes her like he's a cowboy who's about to ride a bull that no one can stay on. Patience is doing some sort of sugar plum fairy dance, bashing everyone in line with her teddy backpack.

"Okay," says Vince, "but you have to do me a favour, too."

"What?"

"Come to my band practice later." He looks at me seriously with his intense blue eyes and then he grins. I melt into a puddle.

Simon watches us warily. I haven't told him that Vince and I met. The line starts to grumble.

"Okay." I blush. I hardly consider it a favour but I was planning to work on my gift for Allison tonight.

I start to walk away and I remember something else.

"Oh, and warn Santa, would you?" Simon is on it. He walks over to Santa, who happens to be Bob (or is it Bob who happens to be Santa?) and whispers in his ear.

I go to the back of the line and fetch Patience, and Simon quietly tells the other parents in line that we have a special needs child who has to go first. They grumble but they seem to accept it, having been treated to a small sample of her behaviour. Patience is the kind of kid that parents thank God they don't have.

"Okay, Patience, let's go. Santa's waiting." Patience grabs my hand and almost dislocates my shoulder getting to the entrance of the North Pole. She takes this opportunity to stick her tongue out at the kids in line.

"Santa hates you!" she yells.

Patience's mom trails behind me and pays Simon. Patience runs to the gate and shrieks, "Where is he? Where's Santa?" Vince grabs her. "Let go of me, you troll! Where's Santa?" We each take an arm and propel her down the fake snowy path and onto Santa's lap. The twinkle in Santa's eye turns a little fearful as she settles in and he completely forgets his standard *Ho Ho Ho!* greeting. Patience elbows him in the belly, struggling to get her teddy bear backpack off to retrieve her list. Vince tries to help.

"Get away from me, you nasty goblin!" she snaps. Vince stands back, hands in the air.

The photographer tries three times to snap a photo while Patience goes through her list, which is written in brown crayon on a roll of paper towels. From where I'm standing, I can see that she's also drawn diagrams and maps. I can also see the word "Italy." Her mom watches from the sidelines, holding Patience's coat and shaking her head. Patience finally jumps off Santa's lap after he's assured her several times that he understands the list. She bolts for the exit, stops and turns around, suddenly zooming in on Vince. She knows the drill.

"Gimme my candy cane!" She stands there with her hands on her hips.

He hands her one with lightning speed and she's off. Her mom dashes behind her to the escalator and suddenly Tornado Patience is gone. We all exhale. They forgot their photos but I guess Patience's mom knows I'll bring them home. The photographer elf shows them to me. In every one of them Patience is a blur. In the only one where you can even tell it's Patience, she's hanging onto Santa's beard with one hand and screaming into his ear. I tell the photo elf to put that one in the cardboard frame with A VISIT TO SANTA written at the bottom. Meanwhile, Vince scribbles an address on a piece of paper and hands it to me. I put it in the pocket of my jeans but I know that later I will remove it, take out the crinkles in the paper and save it forever.

"We start around four, okay?"

I nod, not trusting myself to respond with anything even remotely cool enough.

Simon is watching us again. His eyes are narrowed and he doesn't look happy and I have a feeling that he has something to say about all this. I don't want to hear it. It really isn't any of his business. I know that Simon probably thinks Vince isn't the kind of guy I should be hanging out with, but who is? And besides, just because the two of them wear the same elf outfit every day doesn't mean he really knows him. He's probably never even had a real conversation with him.

It's half-past three when I finally get home from the mall. I rush upstairs and start working on Allison's gift. It's an old faded jean jacket that I bought yesterday at a second-hand store. I washed it four times last night and my plan is to sew some embroidered ribbon around the cuffs and on the collars. I also found an iron-on Elvis Costello patch with the cover of *My Aim Is True* on it that I'm planning to put on the back. He's her favourite rock star, but don't even think of calling him that. She calls him a composer/arranger/musician.

It takes me forever to thread a needle and then I immediately prick my index finger. A small drop of blood appears on my fingertip. I stick it in my mouth but as soon as I take it out the drop of blood reappears. I finally go in search of a bandage. A jean jacket with bloodstains on it just doesn't say "Merry Christmas." I finally find a bandage and I start to sew the ribbon on, but I'm really bad at it and I get a couple of inches along and it looks all crooked. I soon realize that this job will take hours if I do it by hand. Plus, the neglected Elsie is nudging me, wanting a walk or some scratching or I don't know what.

I stand at the top of the stairs and listen. My mom's doing something in the kitchen. I listen for busy noises. I hear a few but not that many so I head down the stairs, holding the jacket. My mom's putting cream cheese into her food processor, her second-best friend after Pam.

"Mom. Can you show me how to do this faster? It's Allison's gift and I have to have it done by tomorrow and I've just been so busy." She puts down a spatula and wipes her hands on a dishtowel.

"Let me look at it," she says. I hand her the jean jacket and the ribbon and show her what I'm planning.

"Oh, honey. That's going to take days by hand. You need to do that on a machine."

By "machine," she means the new sewing machine. It arrived shortly after she decided to "reinvent" herself. A year ago she couldn't even sew a button on. Apparently, reinventing yourself requires sewing skills.

I sigh and shrug. "But I don't have days and even if I did, I don't know how to use the machine." I try to look pathetic.

She thinks a minute. "I'll tell you what. We'll do a trade. I'll sew the jacket on my machine and, since you've become such an expert, you can wrap the gifts. How's that?"

I'm careful not to tip my hand. "All of the gifts?"

"Well, except your own and the ones that are done already."

I try to look like I'm considering this carefully.

"Okay, deal," I say, as though it's even close to fair.

I feel a little guilty since I promised myself I would make Allison's gift, but I did design it and I know she's going to love it. So what difference does it make? I only hope she didn't knit me an afghan or build me a rocking chair.

Now I have to figure out how to get myself over to Vince's.

Chapter 9

"Mom, I'm taking Elsie for a walk!"

I stand at the bottom of the stairs, holding Elsie's leash while she practically does cartwheels. I can hear the gentle hum of my mom's sewing machine as it stops and starts.

"Okay, honey!" she calls.

I still feel a little guilty. My mom is making Allison's Christmas gift while I go off to seek the love of an elf. But for days I have been wrapping gifts until my fingers ache. I deserve this. I open the front door and Elsie bounds out into the snow like a released prisoner.

The address Vince gave me is about twenty minutes from my house, a good walk for Elsie. I'm underdressed for the weather in a turtleneck sweater and down vest but I can't exactly arrive at Vince's dressed like the abominable snowman. If I die of hypothermia along the way and they find my frozen body in a snowbank, well, at least I'll look cool.

Elsie is loving the snow; she's tunnelling, snorting and rolling. She looks back at me every few seconds to see if I'm watching. I walk quickly, my boots making a *crunch crunch* noise on the packed-snow sidewalk. I have to factor in the time I spend at Vince's and try to make it look like a real walk, arriving home before my mom files a missing person's report.

When I turn the corner onto Vince's block, I can already hear the noise, er, music. I wonder how the neighbours put up with it. Elsie cocks her ears. This is her first rock band experience. I guess it's mine, too.

It's pretty obvious that the band practice is in the garage so I walk around to the side door and knock, which seems ridiculous because who would hear me? I finally just open the door and let myself in. Vince is heavy into his drumming thing and he doesn't seem to notice me. Out of his elf costume, he's even more attractive. He's wearing jeans and a black Operation Ivy T-shirt. His hair is sticking out everywhere. He flips his head back and forth and up and down erratically. The guitar player dances around while he tries to get the fingering right. I recognize him from my school. The bass player just stands there, half asleep, calmly plucking strings. I can't really tell if they're any good. If loud is good, they're great. They *look* awfully good, though.

I stand there, trying to look casual. I'm pretty sure my cheeks are bright red from the cold. Elsie sits at my feet, watching. She looks a little frightened and I hope I'm not causing her hearing damage. I'm wondering if I should tap my foot or bob my head. Dancing around seems out of the question, as I've never quite mastered that. The guitar player approaches the microphone and sings, or rather, yells a verse about a highway and a car or maybe a crash, I'm not sure. Then the song ends and it's quiet. I clap but it's barely audible in my gloves. Vince seems to see me for the first time, which is fine by me because

I've had a chance to defrost. He drops his drumsticks and comes over to me, smiling (with his amazing overlapped-tooth smile).

"Hey, you came!" He hugs me and it's over before I can figure out where to put my hands. He smells of sweat and cigarettes and something foody.

Elsie jumps up on Vince and he crouches down and ruffles her fur.

"Who's this?"

"Elsie."

"Hey, Elsie!" He pats her head and stands up.

"I can't stay long," I say. "I have to get my dog home." I have to get my dog home?! Could that sound any lamer?

"That's okay, we can only do a couple more songs any-way. My dad's home in twenty-five minutes and he has to put his car in the garage. He goes ballistic if we're still in here when he pulls up. Why don't you sit over there?" He points to an old vinyl kitchen chair in the corner.

"Okay." Elsie and I settle in and Vince sits back down behind the drums. He has a microphone, too, and he pulls it over to his mouth.

"This next one is for Clare." He winks at me.

I blush.

The song starts off fast and loud and begins to sound a lot like the last one, although this one seems to be about fighting and war. Vince sings backup on the chorus. I can't make out the words but watching his full pinkish lips mov-ing at the microphone is almost more than I can stand.

Elsie nuzzles her face into my leg and I try to casually cover her ears. The next two songs are about girls, I think. I'm starting to feel a little silly just sitting there while this tower of noise keeps coming at me.

Suddenly, Vince looks at the plastic Coke bottle clock above a pile of lawn furniture and the music stops. The three of them turn into an Indie pit crew: unplugging things; rolling up carpet; and moving instruments, cords, amplifiers and microphones across the garage into a neat pile. I stand there, watching. The other two band members grab their guitar cases and they're gone before we're even introduced. I'm starting to think Vince's dad is the big bad wolf or something. Finally, Vince looks satisfied that there's no evidence of a recent band practice and he turns to me.

"Well, I should go," I say. "You guys are really great."

"Yeah, thanks." He runs his hand through his hair. "We need to rehearse more, but you think we sound good?"

"Yeah, really good." I nod vigorously. I want him to believe me.

"We hope to start getting some gigs soon. That would really be cool."

"Great!"

"So, I guess I'll see you on Saturday? Let me get you the address." He pulls a matchbook out of his pocket and pulls the cover off. He roots around in a drawer full of tools and stuff and comes up with a stubby pencil. He thinks for a few seconds and then scribbles an address on the matchbook cover and hands it to me. "It starts at eight but any time's good."

I look at it. It says "Dooky" with an address below it. "Okay. I'll be there." I smile. I guess he won't be picking me up then. Does that mean it's not actually a date? Elsie tugs at her leash.

Vince starts to tap his drumsticks on his pants and look distracted.

"Great. So, bye." I do a half-wave and follow Elsie out the door. As we're heading down the driveway, a black car pulls in. A stern-looking man is driving. The garage door rolls open slowly. It's just a garage now. The man doesn't seem to see me at all as he drives in. The door rolls down again behind him.

The neatly sewn jean jacket is lying across my bed when I arrive home. It's absolutely perfect. She even did the iron-on for me. I add some superhero buttons to the collar and an Elvis Costello button on the flap of the pocket. On the floor next to my bed sits a mountain of gifts with rolls of wrapping paper, tape, scissors, tags and ribbon. I'm suddenly exhausted. My mom is nowhere to be found. So much for hurrying home.

I grab the phone and dial Allison's number. I can't wait to tell her about the band practice. Her mom picks up on the second ring. She tells me that Allison is at the science museum with Paul. After I hang up the phone, I sit on my bed for a minute wondering how I feel about that. Couldn't Allison and Paul have asked me along? I would have said no, but it would have been nice to be asked since it used to be my favourite place to go with Paul, besides the Dairy Delite and Japanese monster films. But how can I possibly feel bad when I haven't even thought about Paul for months?

I jump as the phone rings again. I assume it's Allison, but it's not. It's Simon.

"Hey, Clare."

"Hi. How's the play going?"

"Last performance is tomorrow night. I can't wait."

"You're a very convincing ghost."

"Thanks. You should audition next year. You'd be great."

"Maybe I will," I say. I suddenly remember something I've been meaning to ask him. "Hey, have you ever had an appointment with Ms. Ganz?"

"The misguided guidance counsellor? Yeah, I saw her last year. Why?"

"What did she tell you?"

He snorts. "She told me I should become a doctor."

"Did you tell her you wanted to be an actor?"

"No, I acted like I wanted to become a doctor. What did she tell you?"

"Social services or health care worker or something along those lines."

"That's ridiculous. You don't believe her, do you?"

"Well, no."

"You're an actor, Clare. Don't expect people to understand that."

I sigh heavily and flop back onto my bed.

"Hey, Sylvia and I are having a sledding party on Saturday night. You wanna come?"

I do want to come, but I suddenly remember the party. "I can't. I have to go to another party."

Simon pauses. "Will Vince be there?"

"Yeah, why?"

"Well, it's not that I don't like Vince, I mean he's a nice guy and all, but ..."

"But what?"

"Well. Vince likes to have fun. You know?"

"What's wrong with that? I like to have fun, too."

"Well, Vince's idea of fun might be a little different from yours."

"When did you become my big brother?"

"Look, Clare, just be careful, okay?"

"Sure." I don't know what he means by that.

"You can still change your mind and come sledding with us, you know."

"Thanks, Simon. I'll call you if I do."

I hang up the phone again and sit there thinking. What did Simon mean by "a different kind of fun"? Then I hear the front door open.

"Clare, come help me with these groceries!"

I head downstairs. My mom is carrying two bags in each hand, her purse on her shoulder and two loaves of French bread under her arm. She barely makes it into the kitchen, where she dumps everything on the counter. She looks like she was engaged in serious battle out there.

"There's about a thousand more bags out in the car," she pants. "I lost my list somewhere along the way. I hope I got everything. I can't go back there. It's horrible. Those people are crazy! I caught a woman trying to steal my ham right out of my cart! The only parking spot I could find wasn't even in the lot and I was lucky to get that! Can you go bring the rest of the bags in for me, honey? I need a glass of water."

"Sure. Hey, Mom? Thanks for sewing that jacket. It looks really amazing."

"Oh!" She beams. "You like it?"

This is still pretty new for my mom, this thing where she does "mother" stuff.

"I love it. I really do."

I put on my boots and go out the door. On my first trip with four bags in hand I ask my mom if I can go to a party on Saturday night. This seems like a good time to ask: she's distracted by the shopping ordeal and we just had a great mother-daughter moment.

"Sure, honey," she says, her head in the fridge. She pulls open a container, sniffs it, makes a face and tosses it. "I just need a phone number and a parent's name. Your dad won't be home for dinner so we're having leftovers."

How am I supposed to come up with a parent's name and phone number? How can I call Vince and ask for that information without him thinking I'm a total dork? How am I going to get to this party without my parents knowing?

Chapter 10

Christmas Eve at the mall is the height of desperation. Basically, it's a big game of musical chairs, except the chairs are gifts and when the Christmas music stops, whoever doesn't have a gift is the loser. Most of the people in line to have their gifts wrapped are suburban dads with the unmistakable look of fear in their eyes. Allison knows she has them over a barrel and she's using it to her advantage.

"This is a really beautiful necklace," she smiles. "I'm sure your wife will love it and she'll also be pleased to know that all contributions are helping in the fight against breast cancer."

The man drops a couple of dollars into the collection jar.

"It's a very big fight, sir," says Allison. The man empties his wallet into the jar. Satisfied, she hands him a pink ribbon. "For your wife," she says, smiling.

While we wrap, I ask her about her trip to the science museum with Paul. She looks all dreamy like someone who just went on a date with Johnny Depp or something.

"Paul and I connect on a million different levels," she says, all starry-eyed.

A million different levels? One level or maybe half a level, but a million? I just don't get it. Paul, by the way, hasn't called me once since he's been back. I mean, sure, we don't connect on a million different levels or anything like that but we have known each other for a really long time and a phone call might be nice. I haven't had my usual hour-long daily phone chats with Allison either now that Paul's arrived on the scene. Yes, I do realize that she's standing right next to me as I'm thinking this but those phone chats are really important to me.

I'm waiting for Allison to ask me how the band practice thing at Vince's went but it never happens, so I just tell her. She gets a strange look on her face.

"What's that look?" I ask.

"What look?"

"That look you just gave me. You know the one."

She looks down. "Well, it's just that Simon called to invite me to his sledding party on Saturday night and, um, don't take this the wrong way, but he doesn't think that Vince is the kind of guy you should be hanging around with."

"Sheesh, when did Simon become the leading authority on suitable dating partners? And how is this any of his business? You're all acting like Vince is a convicted felon or something!"

"Don't get mad at me. I don't even know the guy. I'm just telling you what I heard because you're my friend and I care about you."

I look over at Vince as he crouches down to talk to a little girl in line to see Santa. He brushes a strand of hair out of his eyes. My pulse quickens and my stomach does a little somersault. It seems to me that the more people tell me he's bad for me, the more attracted I am to him. What's that all about?

Simon is there too, but visits to Santa have reached a state of all-out panic, so trying to catch his eye for the purpose of glaring at him is out of the question. What I'd really like to do is walk over and punch him in the arm. It must be nice being perfect, looking perfect, having the perfect girlfriend. You get to sit in judgement of everyone around you.

Allison and I are off at four today, leaving poor Betty to deal with the rest of the desperate husbands and boy-friends (I get the feeling that all the women are in a bar somewhere, laughing) until the mall closes at nine. Betty's sister is helping her out. She's a shorter, rounder, calmer version of Betty with the same taste in festive wear. Her name is Millie, but we call her "Betty Lite."

I glance at the North Pole one last time, hoping that Vince will look up at me but his back is to me. I'm really going to miss looking at him whenever I want. On the other hand, I can't wait to get out of this horrible place. If I hear one more Christmas carol, I may have to start throwing things. I can just imagine the headlines: THIRTEEN-YEAR-OLD GIRL GOES BERSERK ON HOLIDAY SHOPPERS.

Allison and I are exchanging gifts at my house later. Better to do it at my house, even though it's a little over-the-top. Her house looks like the Grinch just left with everything. Besides, my parents are going out to a "Gathering" with the "Free and Easy" crowd. My dad tried to get out of it twenty different ways. My mom's making him dress super casual so he won't scare anyone. Allison's parents are invited, too. They're card-carrying, flag-waving members. It all works out perfectly. I need the house to myself because I'm planning on asking Allison a big favour and I can't have anyone listening in.

The last stop at the mall is the record store, the only place where Christmas music is not playing. In fact, I'm not even sure that what's playing could be considered music. It sounds like a choir of angry cavemen. I'm here to pick up a CD for Vince. I follow a guy carrying a stack of CDs for a minute to make sure he works there. When I see that he's putting them away I walk over and ask him for help. He has dyed black hair with blond roots and he's wearing eyeliner. His black T-shirt is torn in a lot of places, as though he put it in the dryer with a cat, and it's held together with big safety pins. He looks like a person who's trying to look scarier than he is.

"Excuse me, I'm looking for something in the Post-Apocalyptic Punk department."

He looks me over. "A gift?" he asks, scratching his head with a spiked silver ring.

"Yes." Gee, I wonder how he figured that out?

"What vintage?"

What vintage? What am I buying here, a bottle of Chardonnay? "Um, I'm not sure."

"Follow me."

I obediently follow behind him. Allison has wandered off to the folk section where things are much simpler. He stops suddenly, pulls out a CD and hands it to me. It's a band called Mars Volta.

"You pretty much can't go wrong with that," he says.

So I plunk down eighteen dollars and ninety-eight cents, more than I spent on Allison's gift. Actually, more than I spent on anyone's gift this year. My reasoning is that Vince could eventually become my boyfriend. It's an investment in my future, a small price to pay, really. I find Allison reading the back of a Joni Mitchell CD. I grab her and we're out of there. The automatic glass doors jerk open and we're home-free. Our work here is done. Mission accomplished. Game over. I may never set foot in this mall again.

Allison and her dog, Elvis, the love of Elsie's life, arrive at my house at 7:00 p.m. I've set the scene with a big bowl of popcorn and a cheese ball with crackers, plus I have hot apple cider mulling on the stove — not just because it smells good, we're actually going to drink it. I ladle it into big mugs and we sit on the oriental carpet in front of the fireplace, surrounded by Christmas overkill. The giant tree twinkles in the corner and stacks of gifts tumble out from underneath it like a rock slide — gifts that I fell asleep wrapping last night. When I woke up, I had drooled all over the gold foil wrap and the outline of a tape dispenser was imprinted on my cheek.

The dogs take turns wrestling each other to the floor. Elvis is bigger and stronger but he tries to play fair and lets Elsie pin him sometimes. Elsie is delusional and believes she's really that tough and walks around like a prizefighter.

Allison opens her gift first because I'm so excited to give it to her that I'm vibrating. She rips the paper off and pulls the box open. She's stunned.

"Wow!" She turns the jacket over to look at the back and immediately pulls it on. It fits perfectly and she looks very cool. "How did you do this? I didn't even know you could sew!"

I shrug. "I just sort of, um, learned."

"I think this is the nicest gift anyone's ever given me. Thank you!"

"You're welcome!" I have to admit, it's a pretty great gift for having pulled it together at the last minute.

"Okay, open yours."

She hands me a big box wrapped in recycled birthday paper. Not surprising: why would there be Christmas paper at Allison's house? I yank open the box and pull out a birdhouse. Not just a plain old birdhouse, but an elaborate, hand-built, hand-painted birdhouse. In fact, it looks just like a miniature version of the house I live in. It has little shutters and windows with window boxes and tiny flowers, and the roof has tiny shingles. It's painted a pretty periwinkle blue with white trim. I can't imagine how long she must have worked on this. She must have started weeks ago, maybe even months.

"Oh, Allison, this is beautiful!"

"It's for the oak tree outside your bedroom window."

"Did you make it in Shop class?" Allison is the only girl taking Shop in our school.

"No. I learned the basics there but I made it at home."

"I love it." I hold it up at eye level. "Now how do I get in this thing? Are you sure you measured right? I know I look small but I'm actually big-boned."

Allison laughs. "I have to confess, my dad helped a bit but I made it mostly myself."

I'm so relieved that she said that. I'm new to this thing where we make gifts. I didn't know if you're allowed to get help. I come clean. "Yeah, my mom helped with the jacket, too."

Allison leans back against the sofa and puts a handful of popcorn into her mouth. I take a sip of cider. I muster up the courage to ask my favour.

"Do you think you could do something for me?"

Allison lies back on the floor and looks up at the tree behind her. "Wow, that tree is massive! How did you get that thing in here? With a crane?"

"I dunno. Allison, the favour?"

"Oh. Sure. What do you need me to do?" She throws a piece of popcorn up into the air and tries to catch it in her mouth. She misses.

"On Saturday night, could you tell your mom that I'm at the sledding party with you?"

"Sure, but why?" She tosses another piece of popcorn and misses again.

"Well, my mom won't let me go to that party unless I get a phone number and a parent's name and everything and I can't very well do that, can I?"

"Why not?"

"You know why not. It's just so uncool."

Allison sits up on her elbows. "Well, we can't have you looking uncool, can we?"

I know what she means and it stings a bit because I know she's right, but I'm not her. I'm not the kind of girl who doesn't care what other people think. I wish I had her courage. I wish I could choose a geek over a jock like she did.

"Can you please just do it?"

"Sure," she shrugs, "I'll do it."

I breathe a sigh of relief but I can't believe I just asked my best friend to lie for me.

"You know I'd do the same for you, right?"

Allison pauses. "Right."

I know what she's thinking. I know she thinks she would never ask me to do something like that. I look at my little birdhouse and I feel a bit uneasy.

Later, after Allison leaves and my parents come home full of eggnog and big opinions, I go upstairs and get into bed.

I feel like I might be heading for uncharted territory with this whole Vince thing. I'm out of my comfort zone but something makes me want to just keep going. I'm really wishing Elsa were here to put things into perspective for me. I put my head down on my pillow and watch Maude swim lazily around the Eiffel Tower in her glass bowl.

Dear Elsa,

It's Christmas Eve and I'm missing you terribly. Remember that guy I told you about? The elf named Vince? Well, I really like him a lot (A LOT) but everyone seems to think I should stay away from him. I'm still going to that party on Saturday night. I'm a little nervous about it. What should I wear? How should I act?

Christmas morning will be strange without you. I'm trying to picture you in Paris on Christmas morning. I'm imagining it might be chilly as you walk along the Seine, wearing your trench coat and a scarf tied so tastefully like the French women are famous for. I really hope you aren't lonely. I hope you're with friends. I miss you.

Merry Christmas,

Clare

Chapter 11

On Christmas morning I wake to the smell of ginger-bread waffles and bacon and coffee — in my opinion, the top three smells on earth. I throw on my bathrobe and make my way downstairs, yawning and scratching, to join my mom and Elsie in the kitchen.

My mom's in full-on Christmas morning mode. A stuffed goose is sitting on the counter in a roasting pan waiting to go into the oven. Elsie guards it from the floor as though it may fly off at any moment. I peek through the glass window on the oven door. A dozen rolls are browning nicely. Somehow my mom is juicing oranges. How is she doing all this without robotic arms? She kisses me on the cheek and hands me a glass of orange juice.

"Merry Christmas, honey. Why don't you set the table for breakfast?"

"Okay." I put my juice down and grab three plates from the cupboard.

"Oh, honey, use the Christmas dishes."

"We have Christmas dishes?"

"They're in the buffet."

"We have a buffet?"

"That wooden thing in the dining room that holds dishes."

I nod. Of course. The buffet. I was thinking "All You Can Eat."

I find the Christmas dishes and carry them into the kitchen. I set them on the kitchen table that's already draped in a festive holiday tablecloth featuring dancing snowmen and Santas.

"Can you go get your dad up for breakfast?"

"Sure." I walk to the bottom of the stairs and yell, "DAD! BREAKFAST!"

"Thanks, Clare. I probably could have managed that myself."

"Don't mention it," I smile.

My dad emerges a few minutes later in his bathrobe, looking a little blurry. He kisses my mom and pours himself a coffee. It's a rare morning that you see my dad at home. The rest of the year he's up at six and gone before I even open my eyes.

"I hate eggnog," he announces, rubbing his head. "Why did you let me drink eggnog? Yuck. It's like liquid quiche."

"I told you not to drink the eggnog. I said, 'Don't drink the eggnog. It gives you a headache.' Remember?"

"When was that?"

"Sit down," says my mom. "I've made gingerbread waffles."

"Are there eggs in that?"

"No," my mom lies.

We eat like cavemen, talking with our mouths full and reaching around each other instead of passing plates. Breakfast takes about seven minutes. There are gifts to open. On Christmas Day, even parents become children.

We rearrange ourselves in the living room with various beverages. My mom and dad have champagne and orange juice and I have hot cocoa. My mom puts on a CD of carols sung by fat, out-of-work opera singers. Then she hands me a small package wrapped in silver paper from under the tree. I tear it open. It's a watch with a black leather strap and a silver face. It has a little button on the side that lights up the face and turns it turquoise so you can tell time in the dark. I actually love it. It's not too girly but it's not too boyish either. Is it possible that she might be catching on?

I give my mom her gift. It's two books by Margaret Atwood. My mom reads now and she's working her way through all the books she missed when she was a lawyer. There's even been talk of joining a book club.

My dad unwraps his gift from me next. It's a tie. It's gold. It's boring. He loves it. I didn't even actually choose it (I would have chosen the one with the bucking broncos on it). My mom chose it and she paid for it, too.

My mom and dad exchange a bunch of gifts, all of which I know they were very specific about when they wrote their lists. I don't understand their gifts. My dad gets stiff shirts, a leather belt (*très* ugly), sweatpants, leather loafers and golf balls. (Quick check: last time he golfed? I think I was nine.) My mom gets sweatpants, sneakers, spa gift certificates and gold hoop earrings (okay, those I kind of like). They both act pretend-surprised. They even say things like, "Ooh, it's just what I wanted!" Duh.

Elsie even gets a stocking full of rawhide chews and biscuits. She gets busy with them immediately.

The pile of opened gifts sitting at my feet also includes sweatpants (two pairs, actually), a leather purse (forget it, that's going back), a bunch of classic movies on DVD, a bunch of T-shirts in totally repulsive colours, a pair of pajamas with different kinds of sushi on them, some makeup designed to make you look like you aren't wearing any, and a hair "system," which basically means shampoo and conditioner.

When we're finished opening gifts, there's a mountain of paper in the middle of the room. Elsie drops her rawhide chew and tunnels into it, ripping the paper to shreds like she's discovered the true meaning of Christmas. We all sit there for a minute watching her and then my mom gets up.

"Well, I guess I'd better get working on that dinner."

I look at my new watch and notice that our family Christmas lasted one hour and twenty-three minutes. I try to remember the last time we all gathered in the living room like this: it was exactly a year ago on Christmas morning.

Promptly at four, a silver sedan pulls quietly in front of the house. The windows are tinted so I can't tell who it is until Aunt Rusty emerges from the passenger's side wearing a fur hat and a long brown sheepskin coat with colourful embroidered edges. The effect is sort of Mongolian sheep herder. She's carrying a large shopping bag. Presents, I presume. A bald man in tiny gold-rimmed sunglasses and a long black overcoat gets out of the driver's side. Gunther, I presume. He looks like a cross between a German hit man and an independent filmmaker. This should be interesting.

Aunt Rusty bursts through the front door without knocking. Elsie attacks and they roll around a bit on the floor while the rest of us look on uncomfortably. She finally stands up and introduces us to Gunther, who politely shakes all of our hands in a way that lets you know that he'd rather not.

"You're so ... on time," observes my mom. Aunt Rusty ignores the obvious dig.

Aunt Rusty hugs me next and pulls her coat and hat off, handing it to my dad like he's the butler. Gunther does the same with his hit man coat. He also takes his sunglasses off and removes a delicate clip from the front of them, transforming them into regular (but still weird) glasses. He carefully puts the clip in a tiny leather case and puts the case in a leather handbag designed for strange European men. My dad exchanges a look with my mom and then hands the coats to her. She disappears behind them. Aunt Rusty flops down on the sofa, making herself right at home.

"I'd kill for a glass of white wine," she says, looking in my dad's direction. She slaps the sofa next to her and I sit down. Gunther chooses the chair that puts him the farthest away from the rest of us while still technically in the same room. He puts his purse on the floor at his feet and then, eyeing Elsie, rethinks it and puts it on a table next to him.

My dad offers Gunther a drink and he asks for a sherry. My dad makes a face; he always says sherry is for old women. But he obediently trots off to look for some. My mom rejoins us, holding a glass of champagne. She digs Aunt Rusty's gift out from under the tree and hands it to her. Aunt Rusty shrieks and tears it open, throwing the wrapping paper on the floor. It's a leather datebook.

"Oh, a datebook, thanks," she says with zero enthusiasm. My aunt isn't what you'd call super-organized. In fact, her arrival on time today was probably all Gunther's doing. I wonder if he's figured out yet that if he stays with my aunt he's in for a lifetime of lateness. My mom likes to buy my aunt little organizer things that she'll never use. She does this to punish my aunt for having too much fun. Last year she bought her a shoe organizer that hangs on a door. My aunt uses it for paintbrushes. I know that my aunt will most likely use the datebook for something like paint samples or a leaf collection, anything but keeping appointments.

My dad delivers the drinks. I give Aunt Rusty her gift: a pair of pink Chinese silk slippers, which she loves. She pulls a box out of her shopping bag and hands it to me. It's wrapped in brown paper that she's hand-painted. I take the paper off carefully. You don't tear hand-painted paper. Inside is a pair of jeans. They're not just jeans, though. They're the softest, coolest, most perfect pair of jeans I've ever seen. The tag inside says that they were made in Italy.

I dash upstairs to my room and slip them on. I stand in front of the full-length mirror on my closet door. I turn around for a look at the back. These jeans have miraculously moved my bum to an entirely different place on my body — a much better place. They feel as though they were sewn by angels with only me in mind. They're snug without being tight, and cool without being slick. I may never take them off. I run back downstairs. Aunt Rusty sucks her breath in when she sees me.

"Oh, honey!" She looks all misty. "I knew it, I knew they were perfect for you."

My mom frowns.

Aunt Rusty gives my mom a tie-dyed silk scarf and my dad a bottle of scotch. Gunther sips his sherry and looks around thoughtfully. He shivers a bit even though he's wearing a black cashmere turtleneck. He carefully brushes Elsie's hair off his clothes. I'm sure that the decor in our house makes him want to gag. He looks to me like his taste probably runs more toward ultra-modern urban chic than the comfy country that my mom favours. I'm picturing a lot of metal and sharp edges. I wonder what he thinks of my aunt's "live-work" space. My aunt is an artist and anything comfortable in her drafty loft is entirely an accident. She's not much of a "nester," as my mom likes to say.

My mom makes uncomfortable small talk with Gunther. She asks where he's from.

"Berlin," says Gunther. He pronounces it "*Baa-lin.*"

"Really?" says my mom. "Is it nice there?"

Gunther shrugs. "It's a *beeg*, dirty, filthy city but *ze* art scene is *kvite* impressive."

My mom nods. The Berlin art scene is not something she's given much thought to in her lifetime.

"And how did you meet Angela?" She steers him back into her comfort zone.

"At a gallery. I *vas* looking at some photographs *und* I saw a beautiful *voman* standing in front of a painting *und* she *vas veeping*."

"Veeping?" asks my dad.

"Yes." Gunther shows him pretend tears by running his index fingers down his cheeks. "*Und* I *vas* so moved that I *valked* over and offered her my *hand-ker-chief*. *Und zen* I asked her to join me for *un* coffee."

My mom looks nauseated and my dad looks skeptical. Not surprising for two people who met in line in the cafeteria at law school. No one's writing *that* romance novel. But I think Gunther's story sounds very romantic. I ask what I think is the obvious question.

"What was the painting of?"

"Clouds," says Aunt Rusty, looking dreamy.

My mom disappears into the kitchen to check on dinner and my dad takes over talking to Gunther. He does about as well as my mom. Gunther takes a pristine white handkerchief out of his pocket and starts cleaning his tiny glasses while he politely answers my dad's inane questions.

Aunt Rusty scrunches down on the sofa next to me and says quietly, "So, what's up with the elf?"

I smile. "I went to his band practice."

"He's in a band?"

I nod.

"Describe him to me."

"Um, well, he's kind of tall with really pale blue eyes, pinkish lips and messy brown hair. One front tooth overlaps the other and when he smiles at me, my stomach does flip-flops."

"Well, of course it does, he's irresistible. When's the party?"

"Tomorrow night," I whisper and then I touch my index finger to my lips and point to the kitchen. Aunt Rusty nods and pretends to be turning a key on her lips. Then she pretends to throw the key over her shoulder.

Our moment is interrupted by someone banging on the front door. I get up and let Patience in. She thrusts a box of chocolate-covered cherries at me. I'm surprised they made it across the street still wrapped.

"Merry Christmas! Open these up and let's eat some."

I manoeuvre her into the living room. She heads directly for the tree and starts shaking the few gifts that are left. I find hers and hand it to her. I picked it out for her myself. She tears it open. It's a pirate costume. Naturally, what she's wearing comes off and she stands there in purple tights and an undershirt with a few stains on it. Gunther has trouble hiding his disgust. He looks at her like she's about to steal his wallet. I help her on with the pirate costume, tying the polka-dot bandana over her unruly red hair and adjusting the eye patch. I show her how to use the hook hand and put the belt with the sword around her waist. There's even a parrot for her shoulder and a fake gold earring. She unsheathes the sword and starts doing a little jig around the living room. Gunther excuses himself and looks for the bathroom. Aunt Rusty loves it and claps. Elsie barks ferociously.

It doesn't take much to get Patience packed up and out the door. She's very big on showing people things and can't wait to get home to show her mom and dad the new look. I close the door behind her and lean against it.

My mom calls us all into the dining room and we find our seats. There's a silver candelabra at either end of the table with pure white candles burning brightly. She walks in carrying a platter with a giant roasted goose surrounded by holly, and sets it in the middle of the long table. We *ooh* and *aaah* and my dad gets up to carve it. If you were to peek in our dining room window right now, you would think we were one of those perfect TV families.

My mom goes back to the kitchen several times and comes out with about a hundred side dishes. Everything looks delicious and I'm starving. Elsie takes her place next to me on the floor with her nose on my knee. We start to pass the food around.

Chapter 12

The more lies you tell, the easier it gets. I heard that once but I'm about to lie to my mom in a major way for the second time in three days and I feel like throwing up. At seven o'clock on Saturday night I pull my old blue jeans over my new premium Italian jeans and put on a scoop-necked, long-sleeved black T-shirt, the most grown-up piece of clothing I own. Over that I pull on a wool turtleneck and a scarf. I get out my backpack and stuff in my down vest, eye shadow, mascara, lip gloss and the CD I bought for Vince. I check my coin purse to make sure I have bus fare and I look at the address on the matchbook cover that Vince gave me for the thousandth time then put it back in the coin purse.

At the front door, I put on my down parka. I can hear my mom and dad talking in the kitchen. I swallow hard.

"Mom, I'm going to pick up Allison for the sledding party!"

My mom appears in the front hallway, licking her fingers. "What time will you be home?"

I bend over to pull on my boots, avoiding her eyes. "I dunno, we're going to Simon's house after but Allison's mom will drop me off."

"Okay." She leans in to kiss me on the cheek. "Ooh, you smell nice."

I swallow again. "Okay, bye. Bye, Dad!"

I hear a muffled "bye" from the kitchen. He's in there eating leftover Christmas dinner.

My mom holds the door open for me. "Be careful! Look out for trees!"

I manage a weak smile as I look back and wave to her. I feel like a lying liar from Liarville.

I crunch through the snow for five blocks to the Dairy Delite. When I arrive there it's practically empty, which I'm grateful for. Not many people crave ice cream the day after Christmas. There's a group of kids in one corner and an old couple in another. The emptiness of the place makes the Christmas decorations and twinkling lights look really sad. I order a Coke from a girl who's hating her job today and slide into the booth where Paul and I sat a million times. This was our hangout. We spent hours at a time here arguing about movies, comic books, whatever. I look out the window and think about how Paul is with Allison tonight at the sledding party and I'm here alone. It doesn't matter, though, I'm going to a party — my first real party — and Vince will be there and it's going to be great.

I take my backpack into the women's bathroom and pull off my old jeans, my down coat, the turtleneck and the scarf. I try not to let anything touch the stained tile floor. I take the makeup out of my pack and apply it carefully, but the light in the bathroom is really dim so I'm not quite sure how it looks. The last thing I do is put the CD into the pocket of my down vest. I mash everything I've taken off into my backpack and walk out the door of the Dairy Delite feeling like a quick-change secret agent. I cross the street to the bus stop and jump from one foot to the other, shivering. The bus finally comes.

Ten minutes later, I get off the bus and walk in the direction of the party. I'm not too familiar with this neighbourhood and I start off in one direction and then realize I'm going the wrong way. I turn around and walk the other way. I find the street and look at the house numbers. When I finally arrive at Dooky's house, I'm numb with cold. The house doesn't look very welcoming but then what was I expecting? A WELCOME CLARE banner?

I walk up the wooden steps and knock tentatively. I can hear music blasting. No one comes to the door. I try the doorknob and it turns easily. I enter a brightly lit foyer filled with hundreds of snow boots. A girl who looks about seventeen watches me with disdain from the top of a small staircase as I bend over to remove my boots.

"Hi," I say.

"Party's downstairs," she points. The big sister, I presume. There's no sign of parents anywhere. Maybe they're out of town and this party is a big sister/little brother negotiation. He gets the party, she doesn't tell. She gets something, he doesn't tell.

I take the stairs slowly. At the bottom I stop for a moment and let my eyes adjust to the darkness. It smells like smoke and there are no lights on except for a couple of lava lamps and a string of Christmas lights hanging on the walls. The music is throbbing. My eyes adjust to the dark and I start to make out faces but I don't see Vince anywhere. I scan the room again and I finally see him leaning against the wall, talking to a girl. When his eyes meet mine he waves and walks over to me, smiling. I've never been so happy to see someone in my life. The girl gives me a withering look.

"Hey, you came!" He hugs me. He smells of smoke and a little bit like beer. The hug lasts a lot longer this time and I'm ready for it.

I put my arms around him and feel his ribs through his shirt. I see the girl over by the wall watching us. Vince talks directly into my ear so I can hear him above the noise. I can feel his warm breath on my neck. He asks me if I'd like a drink and I tell him I'd like a Coke.

"No. I meant a drink."

It suddenly dawns on me what he means by "drink."

"Oh. Um, no thanks, maybe later."

He shrugs and goes off to get me that Coke. I look around at the crowd. A lot of the kids here are older than me. I recognize Vince's bandmates and a couple of other kids who go to my school, but mostly I'm a stranger in a strange land. Vince arrives back with a Coke in his hand. He takes a sip of it and hands it to me.

"Drink up." He winks at me.

I take a sip and notice a funny taste. At first I think it must be my imagination, but I take another sip and before I can think about the fact that there might be something besides Coke in there, someone calls out, "Spin the Bottle, everyone! Sit in a circle on the floor!"

Vince smiles and takes my hand. His hand feels rough and a bit calloused, probably from drumming, I think. I follow him to the centre of the room where everyone is sitting down in a big circle. I'm obviously supposed to have played this before. Everyone seems to know what's going on except me. I sit next to Vince on the floor and he leans into me. I can feel the warmth of his body next to mine and I like it. The girl from the wall is now sitting directly across from me and she's staring at me with daggers. She whispers something to the girl next to her and now I'm getting two sets of daggers.

Someone turns down the music and another person spins the bottle in the middle of the circle. The bottle turns around a few times and stops in front of a pimply blond kid. Everyone in the circle except me yells, "Truth or Dare!" The kid, whose name is Tom, chooses "Dare" and someone in the circle tells him to pick a girl and spend five minutes alone with her in the "make-out room." *The make-out room? There's a make-out room?* My heart starts to pound in my chest. He stands up and picks a girl with long dark hair named Chelsea and the two of them leave the circle together. Everyone hoots and hollers as they leave the room and someone times them on a wristwatch.

While they're gone, everyone speculates on what they're doing. If they're even doing half the stuff that the people in the circle are suggesting, I should probably make a run for it, but Vince is sitting right next to me and I just want to be near him. When five minutes are up, someone yells for the couple to return and they come back to the circle and sit down. Tom is wearing Chelsea's lipstick all over his face and Chelsea's cheeks are bright pink.

The game continues like this and the bottle narrowly misses me each time. No one seems to take "Truth" and the make-out room is seeing a lot of traffic. Finally, the bottle lands on Vince. He chooses "Dare." The last person who was "It" gets to choose the dare. It's a girl with short blonde hair. She tells him he has to spend five minutes in the make-out room with a girl of his choice. Vince's eyes flicker over at the girl across from us and I realize that this must be Vicky, the one Vince's mom mistook me for when I called. My heart is in my throat. Vince takes my hand and I seriously hope I can walk. I follow him into the make-out room. It turns out to be the laundry room with an old easy chair in it. There are no lights at all in this room and I can smell the people who were in it before us mixed with Tide. I really wish I had a breath mint.

Vince doesn't waste any time. He pulls me to him. Part of me loves it and part of me is terrified. This isn't at all how I imagined things unfolding between us. This is the opposite of romance. Before I know it, Vince's lips are on mine. At first he kisses me softly and I start to kiss him back, but he suddenly becomes more aggressive and his tongue slips inside my mouth, surprising me. I pull away and he puts his hands on the sides of my face.

"Don't be afraid," he says gently. "It's okay, it's fun. Just let it happen."

I try to relax. I try to forget that we're in a laundry room and we're playing a stupid game. Vince starts kissing me again and he presses himself against me. His hands travel down my back and onto my new Italian jeans. I hear them calling "time's up" from the other room. I gently try to push him away. "Time's up," I tell him. "We have to go back."

"One more minute," he whispers. His breath is hot on my neck. "C'mon."

They call us again from the other room and I pull away from Vince. He looks annoyed. "I thought you were cooler than that," he says coldly, and leads the way back to the other room. I trail behind him, feeling as though I've been punched in the stomach.

All eyes are on us when we rejoin the circle. Vicky is searching my face for clues and I see her exchange looks with the girl next to her. I'm sure that I don't look happy but I really hope that I don't look afraid. On the next spin the bottle lands on Vicky. Since Vince was "It" last, he chooses her dare: five minutes in the make-out room with a guy of her choice. Vicky chooses him and they leave the circle together. I'm mortified. I look down at the bottle, hoping nobody is watching me. My mouth is dry and it tastes like cigarette smoke and I feel like throwing up for the second time tonight.

Five minutes later — possibly the longest five minutes of my life — Vicky and Vince return to the circle. Both of them are smiling. I want desperately to leave but I'm frozen to my spot on the floor. Vince takes his place next to me again but he keeps his distance and he doesn't look at me. Unbelievably, the bottle stops in front of Vince again. He surprises everyone by choosing "Truth" this time. Vicky gets to choose the question. She thinks for a moment and finally comes up with something.

"Okay, tell us something really, really bad that you've done in the last, uh, let's see —" she thinks about it for a second, "in the last month."

Everyone in the circle laughs and jokes about how that shouldn't be too hard for Vince.

Vince thinks for a moment and then a slow grin creeps across his face. "Okay, I've got one. Are you ready for this?"

Everyone cheers.

"Well, a couple of Saturdays ago, Seth and I got blasted and we went over to BLT and tagged the nativity scene."

Everyone in the circle starts to laugh. The boys high-five him and say things like "Rad" and "Awesome" and "I knew that was you." Vicky looks at him with new admiration.

I stand up slowly and back away from the circle. I turn around and run up the stairs. As I'm fumbling through the mountain of boots, looking for mine, I can hear them laughing and saying things like, "What's wrong with her? Who invited her, anyway? Isn't she an eighth-grader from BLT?"

I pull my boots on and throw my backpack over my shoulder and I'm out the door. As I walk quickly up the street, away from the party, I can feel the sharp edges of the CD I bought for Vince in my pocket.

Chapter 13

I stand at the bus stop, shivering and praying that a bus shows up soon but I don't know the schedule. I really wasn't expecting to leave the party less than an hour after I got there. I may have even had a crazy notion that Vince would walk me home. The minute I felt far enough away from Dooky's house (I never did meet Dooky), I stopped and pulled off my down vest and replaced it with my wool sweater and my scarf and my down jacket from my backpack. I'm still shivering, though, and I'm also crying. I wipe tears and makeup and snot away with my scarf and it's freezing into a solid mass. I don't have any tissues with me. All I feel is stupid, stupid, stupid.

If I had listened to my friends I'd be sledding tonight with people who actually care about me, but instead I'm standing at a bus stop in a strange neighbourhood, crying my eyes out. I can't believe that I thought Vince actually cared about me when all he was doing was populating the party with girls. I'm such an idiot.

By the time the bus arrives, I've mostly pulled myself together, but I sit in the very back and hug my knees to my chest. I feel as though I'll never be warm again. It dawns on me that I'll have some explaining to do if I arrive home so early. I figure I'll just tell my mom that I didn't feel well so I came home.

It takes forever to get back to my neighbourhood. I get off at my stop and walk home slowly. When I get closer to my house I notice that my dad's car is gone but all the lights in the house are on. Maybe he went out to pick up a pizza or a movie. I open the front door and immediately notice that Elsie's not there attacking me. I pull off my boots and walk into the living room. My mom is sitting on the sofa with her feet curled under her. She's bundled up in a sweater. She looks really upset.

"Where's Elsie?" I ask.

"She's at the vet. Your dad took her. Apparently she ate about a pound of chocolate that Patience shoved through the mail slot. She's very, very sick. Get in the car, Clare, we have some talking to do."

I cry all the way to the vet and I tell my mom everything. It's not like she doesn't know already. When they realized that Elsie was really sick, they put her in the car and my dad took her to the vet while my mom drove to the sledding hill to pick me up. I know that Allison did her best to cover for me, but what could she do? I'm a terrible, awful person and now my dog might die!

When we get to the vet, I jump out of the car and run inside. The only other person in the nearly empty waiting room is a woman with a cat yowling from inside a cat carrier. I tell the receptionist that my dog is here and she directs me to the room where Elsie is. My mom catches up with me and we go in together. Elsie is lying on a doggy bed with an IV in her paw. My dad is sitting next to her, stroking her. I lean over Elsie, holding her, sobbing. My dad pats the back of my head. I think that my mom and dad know that whatever I've done, I've already punished myself enough for it.

The vet wants us to leave Elsie there overnight. I beg him to let me sleep on the floor next to her but he says it's not allowed. He promises to call first thing in the morning to let us know how she's doing. He says that she won't be out of the woods for at least twenty-four hours and it was really lucky that someone was at home or she probably would have died.

Back at home the phone machine is blinking. There are messages from Allison, Paul and Simon. They all want to know if Elsie's okay. I'm too ashamed to call anyone. I go upstairs and take a hot shower. I get into bed and my mom brings me a cup of herbal tea. Somehow, I'm still shivering. She sits next to me on the bed and puts her warm hand on my forehead.

"Do you feel okay?"

"I think I might feel better if you grounded me for life."

"Clare, I know that I can seem distracted or busy a lot of the time but I want you to promise me that you'll talk to me about these things in the future. I've always trusted you, but you're too young to make the right decisions for yourself all the time. I don't always know what they are either, but will you please, please promise me that you'll talk to me next time?"

"There won't be a next time." My eyes well up with tears again.

"Of course there will, honey. It always takes a little time to find out what kind of people you want to be with. I'm still working that out for myself." She smiles.

Maybe it's because my mom's so new at being a "mom," but she doesn't pretend to know everything about raising a kid. Sometimes I really appreciate that.

I'm so worried about Elsie that I barely sleep at all. I finally drift off for a while but I wake up suddenly with the feeling that I'm not alone in my room. I feel for Elsie on the bed and remember that she's not there. My digital clock says 4:03 a.m. I sit up on my elbows and look around.

"Hey, over here."

"Elsa?" In the darkness, I make out her profile, sitting in my wooden rocker.

"Get the light, would ya? I feel like I'm in a horror film."

I bend over and click on my bedside lamp.

"What are you doing here?" I rub at my puffy eyes.

"Gads, girl, look at you. You're a mess. You might want to consider cucumber slices for those eyes."

Elsa's wearing a long, soft-looking mauve sweater and knee-high riding boots. Her blonde hair is pulled back into a ponytail and she has gold hoops in her ears.

"How's Paris?"

Elsa yawns. "Paris is okay. It's slushy, it's drafty. The French are brilliant with cheese but not exactly geniuses when it comes to central heating."

"I guess you know all about the Vince fiasco."

"Indeed. Well, not to worry. You're only thirteen and you've suffered your first bad boy. What's the harm in that? I'm going to assume you're wiser for it."

"I don't feel wise, I feel stupid."

"Stupid? Trust me, we've all been there. The guy was adorable. So, you apologize to Allison and you carry on. In France we say, '*Ça ne fait rien*' — it's nothing."

"But I REALLY liked Vince."

"Sure you did, who wouldn't? He's dangerous, gorgeous, appealing in so many ways. Women like us — passionate women — we constantly fall for that. I once fell for an Argentinian polo player who practically wore a name tag that said 'Bad Boy.' Naturally, he tore my heart out, but look at me; I'm back on the horse. No pun intended."

I'm sure Elsa's right. I should just put all this behind me, but somehow I don't think this is something that will go away overnight. I feel like this might take some time to live down. And what about poor, sick Elsie? How can I forgive myself for not being here for her?

Elsa reads my mind. "Don't worry about that dog, either. Although frankly, I don't see what all the fuss is about. She'll be good as new in a few days."

I smile at her. "Thanks, Elsa."

Elsa stretches. "Well, I guess I'm off. You really ought to get some sleep. You look like something the cat dragged in."

I rub my puffy eyes. When I open them again, the rocker's empty. It moves back and forth a bit and then stops.

I finally drift off to sleep again.

I wake up in the morning and lie there a moment. The night before comes rushing back to me like a bad dream. I wish I could take it all back. I wish I'd never met Vince, never gone to that party, never lied to anyone. I roll over and look at the clock. It's almost nine! I hadn't meant to sleep so late. I jump out of bed and rush downstairs to see if my mom's heard from the vet. On the way down, I remember my visit with Elsa in the wee hours. Had I dreamed it or did it really happen? It seemed awfully real.

My mom's sitting at the table eating a bowl of cereal, reading the paper and looking very calm.

"Is she okay?" I ask anxiously.

"She's okay. Get dressed and we'll go visit her."

"Where's Dad?"

"He went to the hardware store to buy a mailbox. We're nailing the mail slot shut. We should have done it months ago."

"The hardware store? Does he even know where that is?" I ask.

"I drew him a map."

I dash back upstairs and throw on my old jeans and a T-shirt. I feel queasy and not hungry at all, but my mom makes me drink a glass of orange juice before we get in the car.

The vet's office is a lot cheerier in the daytime and the waiting room is now a menagerie of pets. Elsie's been moved to a recovery kennel. The doctor opens the metal door for me and I crawl inside with Elsie. She's still lying on the doggy bed but her tail thumps a few times when she sees me. I curl up with her and start to cry all over again. I tell her how sorry I am over and over. The vet says we should call later in the day for a progress report. Leaving Elsie there practically kills me.

Chapter 14

When we get home from the vet I tell my mom I'm going to lie down for a while. I barely make it up the stairs to my bedroom. I fall instantly into a coma-like sleep. All my worries about Elsie and all my shame about the night before disappear temporarily. I wake up feeling groggy. I'm thinking I've slept for about half an hour but when I look out my bedroom window the sun is low in the sky and my clock says 4:12 p.m.

I run downstairs, rubbing my eyes. My mom's in the kitchen, stirring a pot of chicken soup on the stove.

"Hi, honey, you want some soup?"

It smells delicious, but first things first. "Did you call the vet? How's Elsie?"

"I called. She's much better. We can pick her up at six. Sit down."

She puts a bowl of soup in front of me and I realize that I haven't eaten since yesterday. I finish it and my mom fills it again. Chicken soup has never tasted so good.

My mom sits across from me, reading a cooking magazine. I keep waiting for her to re-address the night before, but she doesn't. Every now and then she looks up at me and smiles, which might just be a little bit worse than the "What were you thinking?" speech. She's definitely more diabolical than I've been led to believe. Moments like these make me realize that she must have been a really good lawyer.

"Allison called three times while you were sleeping. She really wants to talk to you." She smiles again.

I make a face.

Six o'clock takes forever to arrive. I can't stand the waiting so I get the place ready for Elsie's homecoming. I gather up all her chew toys and put them next to her doggy bed. I vacuum her doggy bed. I clean out her food bowl and her water bowl until they sparkle. I find all her leashes and hang them next to the front door. I fill her glass biscuit jar with fresh biscuits.

This time Elsie greets me at the door of her kennel. The vet lets her out and she walks gingerly over to us. I hug her. The vet tells us that it'll take a few days before she's herself again and she has to go back to puppy food for a while. All the way home in the car, I hang on to Elsie for dear life.

When we arrive home, my dad has mounted the new mailbox next to the front door. It's a shiny brass deal. I'm beyond impressed to see that my dad not only found the hardware store but actually returned home with a bag of hardware and then installed the aforementioned hardware. What could possibly be next? Checking his own oil?

Apparently, Patience came over for a little talk about why the mail slot won't open any more. Since she can't reach the new mailbox, we're hoping that the "special deliveries" might stop altogether.

I carry Elsie upstairs to my room and put her on my bed. She stretches and yawns and goes directly to sleep. I kiss her on the head several more times. I've kissed her so many times that her head smells like cherry lip balm.

I grab the phone and dial Allison's number. Allison is not only miraculously at home, she's been waiting for me to call. I lie down on my bed next to Elsie with the phone and spill all the details of the night before. I squint with embarrassment as I tell her, because in this version I sound even stupider. Allison is one-half supportive friend and one-half raging feminist. The supportive friend half wants me to feel better and move on and the feminist half wants to figure out the most painful, creative way to kill Vince. I don't want to kill anyone but I'm so grateful for her support.

Allison and I make a date to get together the next day. I'm okay leaving Elsie because the vet said we should let her sleep as much as she wants. I think that might apply to me, too. I eat a quick dinner with my mom and dad and then I go back to bed with Elsie next to me. I sleep with my arm draped over her, waking up every hour to check on her.

Elsie wakes up bright and early in the morning looking like a brand new dog. She looks like she might be thinking, "Hey, where'd I go? What happened?" Her nose is wet and cold, her eyes are clear, she's hungry and she wants everyone to snap to the new program.

I feed her and take her outside in the backyard where she tackles me like a champ. The relief I feel is unbelievable. Elsie's whole again.

Chapter 15

The record store employee with the black eyeliner and the ripped clothing looks at me with a level of interest reserved for the Tragically Unhip. He's about as happy to see me as I am to see him. I wasn't planning on being back at the mall so soon.

"You're returning this?" He looks down at the Mars Volta CD sitting on the counter between us.

"Yes."

"I'll be in the Elvis section," says Allison. She means Costello, not Presley.

"It's a pretty righteous CD," he says.

"Yeah. Well, he already has it."

"That's cool." He nods his head a few times. "I can only give you store credit, though."

"Fine."

He writes me a credit slip in his serial killer hand-writing and I take it from him and walk away from the cash register. Allison is wearing earphones and she's deeply engrossed in the cover of the new Elvis Costello. Allison is the kind of girl who will wait for it to come in to our local library instead of buying it. I grab a copy of it from a display and slap it down in front of scary record store guy. He looks at me with exactly the same level of interest as before.

"Can I help you?" he asks.

Is it possible that he doesn't remember me from four seconds ago?

"Yes. I'd like this." I slide the credit slip over the counter.

He sighs and takes the slip, checking it for authenticity, as if he didn't just write it. He slides the CD into a bag and hands it to me.

"Thanks," I say, taking the bag.

"You bet," he says, which is record store talk for, "Go away."

I walk over and tap Allison on the shoulder. She spins around and smiles. She takes the earphones off and puts them on me. I recognize the rich guitar sound and then the voice of Elvis Costello. It's a cool song. I listen for a bit and take the headphones off.

"That's great. Let's get out of here. Goth Guy wants me dead."

We walk back out into the mall. The North Pole is completely deserted. Somehow it depresses me. Maybe it's because, back when Vince was an elf, I imagined so much more for us. Shoppers have returned to the mall in droves, carrying bags of unwanted gifts to return to the store.

I hand the little bag to Allison.

"What's this?" she asks.

"Nothing, just a little present."

She pulls the Elvis Costello CD out of the bag. "Wow! What'd you do that for?"

"Because you never once said, 'I told you so.'"

She smiles and kisses the cover of the CD. "Thanks!"

On the way out of the mall I spy a sign on a little shop that says EAR PIERCING $14.95. I suddenly feel like doing something reckless and impulsive.

"Al, how much money do you have on you?"

"Um, probably about five bucks, why?"

"I think I have about ten bucks and some change. Can I borrow your five bucks?"

"Sure, why?"

I start off toward the shop, grinning at Allison.

"You're not!"

"Why not? You got your ears pierced."

"Yeah, but I was a three-year-old love child of hippie parents and I have no memory of the pain. Besides, I practically never wear earrings."

"I'm going in." I pull open the door.

A girl who looks like she's probably dating Goth Guy from the record store reluctantly puts down her graphic novel to see what she can do for me. Judging by the number of piercings on her face, I would say that she's had a lot of practice — and those are just the ones I can see.

"Hi," I say. "I'd like to have my ears pierced."

She looks annoyed and hands me a form. "Fill this out. Are you fourteen?"

I toy with lying about my age but then I remember that lying hasn't been going so well for me lately. "No, thirteen."

"If you're under fourteen, you need permission from a parent or guardian. Take the form home and have them sign it."

Allison looks up from a rack of temporary tattoos. "Uh-oh."

I think fast. I may not be so brave tomorrow. The whole point of acting reckless is doing something immediately. Forms and permission and signatures just don't figure into this plan.

"Hey, how about if I get my mom on the phone right now? Would that work?"

She stares at me a moment and then she hands me a phone.

My mom picks up on the third ring. "Hi, Mom. Can I get my ears pierced?"

"Can we talk about this when you get home?"

"No, actually. I'm at the ear-piercing place and I need your permission. Allison's mom let her get hers done."

"Today?"

"No, a while ago." Allison snorts and holds up three fingers. I wave her away.

"I thought we were going to wait until you were fourteen. Isn't that what we decided?"

"So I do it six months before I'm fourteen, what's the big deal?"

She sighs. "Who's doing it?"

"A woman. I think she might be a nurse, actually." The girl looks at me in alarm. I know that this is also technically a lie but it's a fairly harmless one and at least now I know the difference. I try to picture her as a nurse. The closest I get is a *Rocky Horror Picture Show* nurse.

"Let me talk to her."

I cover the receiver with my hand. "Would you mind pretending to be a nurse?"

She glares at me and takes the phone.

"Hello?" she says. "Yes. I've done this a lot. It's very safe."

"Yes, we sterilize everything."

"No. I've never seen anything like that. Everyone I've pierced is still alive."

"Okay."

"Okay."

"Okay." She's starting to look exasperated.

"Sure." She hands the phone back to me.

"Hi, Mom."

"I said it was okay, but I want you to come home right after it's done and only the ears. No noses or navels or eyebrows or lips and don't touch your ears with dirty fingers."

"Okay. Thanks, Mom."

I hang up the phone and the "nurse" gives me a choice of earrings. For $14.95 I'm pretty limited. I choose little silver hoops. Goth Girl points to a stool. I sit down and Allison comes over to watch. Goth Girl rubs my earlobes with a numbing solution that stinks. Then she draws a dot on each earlobe with a pen and stands back to see if they match up. She pulls out a piece of equipment that looks a lot like a nail gun. She loads one of the earrings onto it and comes at me with it. The sensation of the earring going through my ear feels like how I imagine it might feel if you stapled your ear with a stapler. Allison goes a little pale. Goth Girl does the other one and I'm done. It took all of three minutes.

We pull out all the money we have and put it on the counter and she hands me a tube of ointment and some instructions. I look at myself in the mirror. My earlobes are bright red. I resist touching them. My fingers are probably really dirty.

Allison and I exit the automatic glass doors again. It's one of those rare melty winter days where the sky is brilliant blue and the sun bounces off the snow and melts the icicles and water drips everywhere. We walk the eight blocks home, a long walk when it's real winter weather, but today there's a tiny taste of spring that's not due for months. My ears start to throb once the numbing stuff wears off. Goth Girl warned me about this and said they would be "tender" for a few days. I'm smart enough to know that that really means, "Your earlobes are going to be killing you for a while."

Now that Allison knows everything about the Vince incident, it appears she's been fuming non-stop. "Are you going to turn him in?" she asks.

"For what?" I ask, dodging a puddle.

"For tagging the manger?"

"Nah. I'm not a snitch. Besides, the way I bolted from the party? He'd know it was me. I'd feel even dumber."

"Yeah, you're probably right. Well, don't worry, he'll probably die of lung cancer."

"That'll teach him." We walk past a sad, drooping snowman in someone's front yard. "Hey, how are things going with Paul?"

"Well, you were right, he *is* the world's worst athlete, but I don't care. The last thing I need is another jock in my life. Paul's really smart and I love talking to him. I could talk to him forever."

I feel a pang of jealousy. I used to be the one Paul talked to. It's true that we never really talked about anything personal, but I guess I never imagined that one day he would replace me with my own best friend. It feels awfully strange. I suppose that's what you call irony: I lose the friend I spent all my time with and then he comes back to town and falls in love with the person I replaced him with — well, maybe not in love, but judging by the look on Allison's face when she talks about him, it's a lot more than "like."

"Hey, you know what? Paul has this friend from school and he lives around here somewhere. Paul says he's really nice. You want me to set up a double date? We could go to the movies or something."

I consider this for a minute. I'm certainly ready to leave Coolville (Cruelville, actually), where I failed miserably, but do I want to go all the way back to Geekville? Isn't there anything in between?

"Nah. I think I'm going to stay away from boys for a while. Besides, my dog almost died. I should probably focus on her for now."

Allison shrugs. "Think about it."

"I will."

"Hey," she says, looking at my earlobes, "your ears aren't quite so red. They look pretty good."

"Thanks." Again, I resist the urge to touch them.

We part ways at the end of my block and I walk alone the rest of the way home.

Chapter 16

In theory, the week between Christmas and New Year's is a great idea. It's a time to regroup, see friends, play with your new stuff, things like that. But when you're thirteen and you've just had your heart broken by a no-good, thoughtless, horrible, awful but gorgeous person, the days can stretch out forever in front of you, leaving you with way too much time to think.

After moping around for most of the afternoon, I clip Elsie's leash on and take her out for a walk. She's still a little "off her spot," as my mom likes to put it, so we stay on the sidewalk rather than going down to the ravine trail like we usually do. I keep Elsie on her leash and try to make her heel, something that she's particularly bad at. Everything that melted yesterday is now frozen again. The sidewalk is a skating rink. The blue sky has also disappeared and now it's as grey as my mood.

My ears are killing me. I can feel them throbbing as I walk. If I bend over to pull my boots on or something, it feels like my earlobes are going to explode. I'm really glad I got them pierced, though. Besides the fact that I've wanted to for a while and Elsa got hers done right after she moved to Paris, I feel like the pain is important; like some sort of weird primitive need to mark myself so that I won't forget the last few days. Like a rite of passage from stupid to enlightened.

Before we left the house I called Allison to invite her and Elvis along, but her mom said she was out with Paul somewhere. "Out with Paul Somewhere" is where I used to go. I hate myself for counting the days until Paul goes back to school (six).

Elsie and I head toward downtown. We're moving pretty slowly because of the slippery sidewalks. If Elsie weren't a little under the weather, I'd be dragged for blocks. We pass the Dairy Delite and I automatically glance inside. Allison and Paul are sitting in the booth I've shared with Paul hundreds of times — the same one I sat in on Saturday night.

I stop and watch them for a minute. Allison takes a spoonful of her ice cream sundae and heads toward Paul's mouth with it. I can't believe I'm seeing this. He's always told me that he's lactose intolerant! I've only seen Paul eat ice cream once and it was boring old vanilla and he spent the rest of the day clutching his stomach and groaning. Paul happily lets Allison shovel the ice cream into his mouth. I suddenly get embarrassed, like I'm watching something very intimate and private. I wait for Paul to fall to the floor, writhing in pain, but he smiles and licks his lips. I storm across the street and away from them.

As I'm walking along the sidewalk grumbling under my breath, we pass a group of girls with skates thrown over their shoulders. I recognize them from school. Some of them are Ginny's "ladies-in-waiting," temporarily relieved of their duties while Ginny's away. They're laughing and talking and enjoying themselves. Is absolutely everyone having a good time except me?

We walk about six blocks before I realize that we're heading toward my school. In fact, we're fast approaching the diner where the cast of *Macbeth* used to go after rehearsals. It's a greasy spoon with bad service and horrible food but I loved it because Simon had insisted that I join the rest of the cast there and he made me feel like I belonged. Even my Drama teacher, Eric, would join us sometimes.

I walk past the front window of the diner. The place is practically deserted. There's one person sitting alone in a booth. He's staring into his coffee cup. It takes me a few seconds to realize that it's Vince. My heart leaps into my throat. I yank Elsie's leash back and scurry behind a tree so Vince can't see me. I stand there watching him, my heart pounding like mad. He looks sad, or maybe thoughtful. It's hard to tell from behind. What kind of a fourteen-year-old sits in a diner alone drinking coffee? Elsie watches me curiously, her head tilted to one side.

Vince is playing with an empty sugar packet. Maybe he's thinking about how horribly he treated me and he's feeling really badly. Maybe he thinks he should call me and apologize. He's probably working out what he's going to say, trying to find the right words. Maybe I should go inside and hear what he has to say, make it easy on him.

Just as I'm looking for a place to tie Elsie's leash, the glass door at the other end of the diner opens and a girl with blonde braids carrying a Scooby-Doo lunchbox purse walks in. She saunters over to Vince's booth and sets the lunchbox down on the table. Vince smiles up at her — that devastating smile — and skootches over. She slides in next to him and plants a kiss squarely on his full lips.

I yelp and drop Elsie's leash. She smells freedom and takes off up the sidewalk in the opposite direction of home. Apparently, she's feeling much better.

"Elsie, no!" I scramble after her. I run past the glass diner window. Suddenly, my legs go out from under me and I land hard on the slippery sidewalk. Now I'm splayed out in full view of Vince and the stupid girl and anyone else in the vicinity. I refuse to look at the diner window but I'm pretty sure that they're enjoying the show. I call out to Elsie again and she turns around. Seeing me on the ground like that seems to interest her (maybe it's time to wrestle?) and she runs back to me and licks my face as I clumsily try to get to my feet. I brush myself off and pretend that I'm fine even though I've probably broken a hip. I grab Elsie's leash and limp off across the street.

Can a person die of humiliation? Is there a limit to how much humiliation a body can endure before the organs just start shutting down, one at a time, and you go into a "humiliation coma," never to awaken again? When they finally pull the plug and you stop breathing, the death certificate reads: CAUSE OF DEATH: HUMILIATION.

Also, it seems awfully strange to me that I grew up in this neighbourhood and never ran into Vince anywhere. Years of living a few blocks apart and I don't see him once, and then suddenly he pops up at my diner like a land mine or a flesh-eating virus. And how is it that he can still make my heart leap after everything he put me through? I consider this as I walk carefully along the sidewalk, feeling like I'm a hundred years old. Elsie is now miraculously well behaved as though she's taking pity on me, or maybe she senses that I could snap at any moment.

I feel that the best plan of action at this point is to head home, run a hot bath and submerge myself in self-pity. In fact, they should make a bath foam called "Self-Pity" for moments like this. What was I even thinking leaving the house? I should have just stayed home and finished off the chocolate Santas and mixed nuts.

Ever since Saturday night, my mom looks really pleased to see me return home from anywhere. She gets this look of relief when I walk through the front door like she's really grateful that I haven't run off and joined the circus or a bike gang or something. I suppose I can't blame her. I tell her that I fell on the ice and I need a hot bath. I make myself a peanut butter sandwich and some herbal tea and take it upstairs into the bathroom, where I turn on the bathtub taps and add my mom's expensive bath foam. I get the phone and put it next to the tub. I take off my clothes and look in the mirror at the ugly purple bruise spreading across my right hip. It hurts when I touch it.

After I get into the tub and adjust the water temperature, I dial Aunt Rusty's number. I'm so relieved that she picks up and not Gunther.

"Hello." She sounds impatient.

"It's me, Clare."

"Clare. What's up, dollface?"

"I'm feeling very humiliated. Can I come over?"

"Sure, when?"

"Um, how about tomorrow?"

"Sure, I'll be painting but we can visit."

I'm the only person allowed in the room when my aunt is working.

"Is Gunther around?" I probably should have asked this before I invited myself over.

"No. He went to Berlin. He's in a custody battle with his ex-wife."

"He has kids?"

"No. A Russian wolfhound named Sasha."

"You mean a dog?"

"Yup. I know it sounds pretty weird but when I suggested he just get a new dog he looked at me in horror. Apparently, this 'Sasha' creature isn't just any old dog."

"What do you mean? Is she like Lassie or something? Did she drag him from a burning building?"

"No, but he mentioned something about her being able to tell the difference between Russian caviar and domestic caviar."

"Well, that is pretty special. I can see how that would come in awfully handy."

"Yeah, can you believe it? Oops, I've got another call coming in. It's probably Gunther. What time tomorrow?"

"Um, noonish?"

"Okay, see you then. Mwah!"

I click the phone off and slide my body down into the tub until my head is underwater.

Chapter 17

Aunt Rusty runs her hands through the greenish-black paint and smears it onto the canvas in front of her. I'm confident that when the painting is finished it will actually look like something, but right now it looks like primordial ooze. She's wearing a New York Dolls T-shirt with the sleeves cut off and torn jeans. She's also wearing a baseball cap turned around backwards with a red ponytail sticking out the back. She's not wearing any makeup except for her trademark bright red Chanel lipstick. She's been wearing it for years and wouldn't think of switching brands. Everything my aunt is wearing is caked in paint. In fact, everything in my aunt's loft has paint on it: the doorknobs, the fridge, the light switches, the phone, the drawers, even the lever that flushes the toilet.

I'm sitting on the floor, leaning against the opposite wall of the loft, watching my aunt paint. There's a giant bag of M&Ms between my legs and I'm eating one after the other. Just being here somehow makes me feel less wretched. I'm not sure why. I think that I somehow take comfort in my aunt's chaos. My ears don't hurt much today and Aunt Rusty has dazzled me with talk of all the fabulous earrings she's going to loan me.

Beethoven is playing on the stereo. My aunt, as a rule, does not listen to classical music so I figure this must be more of Gunther's influence. I also noticed when I opened the fridge that there's actual food in it, a foreign concept to my aunt. There are three apples, a block of cheese and even milk; it looks like Gunther placed everything in there carefully to make it look like a still life painting. My aunt doesn't know that milk comes from cows; she thinks it comes from the Italian café up the street. When she's hungry, she calls one of the numbers on the stack of menus she keeps by the paint-spattered phone and *voilà*! — a delivery guy shows up with a bag of food. She's the only person I know of who buys birthday gifts for the Chinese food delivery guy. There's a drawer in her kitchen filled with about three thousand pairs of wooden chopsticks and about the same number of little soy sauce packets.

Aunt Rusty wipes her hands on a rag and grabs a large paintbrush. She stands there, looking at the canvas for a minute. We're rehashing yesterday's chain of events. I'm not sure that's healthy but my black-and-blue hip is throbbing non-stop anyway, reminding me of it every minute, so who cares?

"So, he's sitting there, waiting for a girl, and you just happen to walk by?"

"Yes. Can you believe it?"

"And this girl. What did she look like?" Aunt Rusty digs through a large tomato juice can of brushes.

"Cute. Blonde braids, great clothes, carrying a cool lunchbox purse. Your basic nightmare."

"Man, that is just so brutal."

"I know. Even if I wanted to compete, I wouldn't stand a chance."

"Well, of course you would if Vince were seeking quality over quantity, but he's not. Vince is one of those guys that you have to survive to get to the good ones. Think of him as a character-builder. Mine was named Raphael. I was *so* in love with him. I wrote his name on the bottom of my sneakers and carried his yearbook picture in my wallet. He deserted me at a school dance for a girl named Marsha."

"Marsha?"

"Yup. We called her 'Marsha the Martian' because she had these huge eyes and no one ever saw her blink. Anyway, it took me months to get over that guy. The weird thing is, after he humiliated me, I became even more obsessed with him." Aunt Rusty starts to move paint around the canvas with a big brush.

"I know what you mean." I throw a brown M&M back in the bag. I don't eat the brown ones.

"Don't worry, sweetie. Eventually this will pass and you'll look back and wonder what the attraction was."

Maybe Aunt Rusty's right, but I remember how my heart jumped into my throat when I saw Vince yesterday.

Aunt Rusty squirts a tube of lime green paint onto the garbage can lid she uses for a pallet. She finds a skinny brush and dips it into the paint, mixing it with a little black.

"You know what you need?" asks Aunt Rusty with her brush in midair.

"No, what?"

"You need a distraction."

"A distraction? What kind of distraction?"

"Well, that's up to you. I always do something completely new, something that demands all your concentration and takes you out of your routine. Like, remember when I took African basket weaving?"

"That was because of a guy?"

"Yup, his name was Terrance. He was a novelist. Remember belly dancing?"

"Vaguely."

"That was Joseph. He was a sculptor."

"What about when you took welding?"

"That was just because I wanted to learn how to weld. There was no guy in that scenario."

"Oh."

Aunt Rusty dabs the lime green onto the canvas. "So, let's think about a distraction for you."

"Okay."

"How about ballet?"

"No. I tried that when I was seven. I'm not ballerina material."

"Okay, how about boxing?"

"Too violent. Mom would never go for it."

"Glass-blowing?"

"Too hot."

"Folk dancing?"

"Absolutely not."

"Circus arts?"

"I'd kill myself."

"How about martial arts?"

"What kind of martial arts?"

"Well, my friend Mavis does tae kwon do and she loves it."

"Hmmm. Let me think about that one." I picture myself in one of those white outfits, delivering a satisfying kick firmly to the solar plexus of a boy with pale blue eyes. He winces in pain. It's very appealing to me.

The painting is slowly becoming something. Now it's a faceless woman sitting on a chair, looking down at her hands. How did I not see that before? I watch without talking for a while. It's amazing how Aunt Rusty can go from looking like she has no idea what she's doing to looking like a genius in a matter of hours. I wonder if there was a Ms. Ganz in her life, trying to move her away from becoming an artist. Knowing Aunt Rusty, she probably would have skipped the appointment or forgotten about it altogether.

Eventually the afternoon sun starts to dip behind a big warehouse across the street. The light in the loft changes to soft shadows. Aunt Rusty stands back and surveys her work. She turns to me, wiping her hands again.

"Well, that's it for my light. You hungry?"

I look down at the bag of M&Ms, now half empty. "Sure, starving."

"Let's order some moo shoo pork."

Chapter 18

Later that night, I'm standing in front of a tae kwon do studio, casually casing the joint. Elsie's my foil. I pretend to be fussing with her leash or having an earnest conversation with her while I look in the window at the students. She's having none of it. This stationary thing is just not for her.

I got the outfit right: white pajama-like things with belts in blue, red or black. The students are paired off and a small but tough-looking Asian man seems to be calling the shots. The couples spar very gracefully. No one seems to be getting hurt and they're all very polite. I imagine them saying, "Hello. Nice to meet you. Would you mind terribly if I kicked you in the head?"

The room is quite empty except for mats on the floor and a narrow wooden bench running along one of the walls. It seems very peaceful and clean and uncluttered — the type of place where it's easy to focus.

A tall thin boy with wavy black hair is doing some very impressive kicking things. He wears a black belt and he's easily the most advanced student in the class. He moves like he could be cast in *Crouching Tiger, Hidden Dragon*. You'd never guess that to look at him, though. His pajamas are too short in the arms and legs, and his exposed wrists and ankles are bony and fragile-looking. He's awfully pale and he stoops a bit, like someone who's been too tall his whole life. Like me.

The boy glances over and catches me watching him. I move away from the window. It's starting to steam up anyway. I take a brochure from the plastic box attached to the door. Inside is a list of classes. There's a beginner's class starting next week; now I just have to decide if this is the kind of distraction I'm looking for. I wonder how long it takes to get a black belt? Years maybe. Do I need to be distracted for years? I was sort of thinking months, even weeks.

When I get home there's a sticky note on the fridge from my mom that says I should call Allison. *And to what do I owe this honour?* I muse. I guess Paul must be busy.

Elsie and I run up the stairs and dive onto my bed. I grab the phone and dial Allison's number. Elsie rearranges my covers into a doggy bed and plops down with a sigh. Allison picks up on the third ring. I'm so happy to hear her voice. Frankly, I was getting a little tired of talking to her mom.

"It's me," I say. "Remember me?" When did I get so needy?

"Hey. Where've you been?"

"Where have I been? Right where you left me."

"Sorry about that. I really am. Paul's leaving Sunday so ... well, you know."

"Sure, but you do remember that I was his friend first."

"Yeah, actually that's why I called. Have you made any plans for New Year's?"

The fact is I haven't given New Year's any thought at all. Why, in my current condition, would I want to dwell on a holiday that, above all other holidays (even Valentine's Day), separates the winners from the losers? Oh, goody, another New Year's with no one to kiss at midnight. I couldn't feel more special.

"Well, let's see, I was thinking of jetting off to Times Square to watch the ball drop but that's *so* 'been done,' so I guess I have no plans."

"Well, Paul and I were thinking that we could come over to your house, rent a Woody Allen classic, get some pizza, you know, that sort of thing."

"Okay. I'm pretty sure my parents are going out, but let me make sure."

"Great, and one more thing."

"Sure."

"Paul wants to know if he can bring Joshua, his friend from school."

"Do I smell a set-up? I don't know, Allison," I sigh.

"No, no, nothing like that. Paul just wants the two of you to meet."

"I'm still stinging from my last close encounter with a boy."

"Vince is a jerk. Joshua's not a jerk."

"Have you met him?"

"Well, no, but Paul says he's great."

"Paul thinks botulism is great."

"True. But what could it hurt? If you don't like him, you don't like him, but if you do ... well ..."

"What if he doesn't like me?" I ask.

"What's not to like?" She says this with a New York accent.

"Let me think about it, okay?"

"Sure."

"Hey," I ask, "do you know anything about tae kwon do?"

"No. Is it like karate?"

"Well, same pajamas, but it's different."

"Are you thinking about taking it?"

"Maybe."

"Cool. Well, I have to call Paul back and let him know we're on. Call me when you make up your mind about Joshua."

"I will."

I click the phone off and stare at the ceiling for a while. Am I ready to meet someone new? I guess there's an upside. If I don't like him, he's leaving Sunday anyway and he won't be back till the summer. So, on the other hand, why even bother? Why open a whole new can of worms? (And where did that phrase come from? Yech!)

I see a flutter of white out of the corner of my eye. Elsie lifts her head and growls softly. Suddenly Elsa appears in full tae kwon do pajamas. Very authentic, except her belt is a floral silk scarf. She kicks her way across the carpet.

"I love this stuff. It keeps me centred," she says, bouncing on the balls of her feet. She takes another kick and knocks my bedside lamp to the floor.

"Oops."

Elsie barks.

"Shut up, furball!"

"You have no idea what you're doing."

"Yes, I do. I watched a video I bought on the Home Shopping Network. Why haven't we done this before? It's fantastic."

She does a few more fancy pretend kicks, sparring with an imaginary partner, and collapses into my rocker.

"I'm exhausted." She looks down at her outfit. "The clothes are icky, though. White after Labour Day? And all monochromatic?" She wags her finger. "I had to jazz it up a bit." She touches the silk scarf around her waist and looks over her shoulder at me coyly. "It's Hermès."

"It's beautiful."

"So, are we doing this or not?"

"Doing what?"

"This! Tae kwon do!"

"I don't know. I think so."

"You think so? Look, it'll be great for your acting, it will teach you focus and meditation, and I'm guessing that the boy/girl ratio is way heavy on the boy side. Plus, you'll be able to defend yourself in dark alleys."

She is right. "Okay, I'll do it."

"Great. Now, about Joshua."

"What about Joshua?"

"Don't you remember our 'Get Back on the Horse' talk?"

"So, in this scenario, the horse is Joshua?"

"Well, yes, but in a very abstract sense."

"I see."

"All I'm suggesting is that you meet the guy. What could it hurt? If you don't want to commit to New Year's, have Allison set it up so that you accidentally-on-purpose bump into him and Paul somewhere so you can size him up ahead of time."

I nod. "That's actually a pretty good idea."

"So say yes. Make it worth my transatlantic journey."

"Okay, okay."

"Sheesh, my job just gets harder and harder and now I have to deal with that furball every time I drop by." She gives Elsie the evil eye. "Well, I'm off. Try to keep an open mind and let me know how it all plays out."

She's gone before I remember to ask what her plans for New Year's are.

I dial Allison's number again.

Chapter 19

Allison is enthusiastic about the drive-by (or rather, walk-by) plan to check out Joshua. I realize that this is a deceitful ambush and if I knew someone was doing this to me I would be horrified, but I can't spend New Year's with a big geek after what I've been through. I'd rather be alone. Superficial? You bet. But I just don't care.

We've arranged to accidentally bump into Paul and Joshua at a bookstore in our neighbourhood at two o'clock. Paul is supposed to be in the graphic novel section of the store. I have serious doubts about Paul executing this simple plan. His attention to detail can be a bit spotty unless he's splitting the atom or determining the square root of numbers in the billions.

Allison picks me up at one-thirty and we make our way over to the store. On the way, I try not to get my hopes up. I tell myself that either way, I don't really care what this Joshua guy turns out to be like. I tell myself that I'm perfectly happy being on my own. Besides, since the Vince incident, my heart has been packed on ice in a cooler under my bed for safekeeping.

I've put zero effort into my appearance today. My hair hangs in oily strings and I'm wearing a sloppy sweater and blue corduroys tucked into my boots. Allison was quick to tell me that I look like a refugee, which is big talk for someone who shops at Goodwill. I thanked her and told her that was the look I was shooting for.

I'm not sure why I wouldn't want to look attractive for Joshua. Maybe a part of me wants to sabotage the whole thing before it even has a chance to get off the ground.

Allison chatters on about Paul as we walk. Sometimes I think she forgets that, until six months ago, I was Paul's only friend and I probably know more about him than she does. I let her ramble on, though; it's a good distraction for me. Even though I could never in a million years think of Paul romantically, I always thought of him as a good friend and I'm struggling with the idea that maybe we were just passing the time together until something — or someone — more meaningful came along.

About halfway to the bookstore Allison pulls off a mitten to scratch her nose and I see a flash of silver on her middle finger.

"What's that?" I point to a ring I've never seen before.

"It's from Paul. It's a Celtic knot."

"You're engaged?"

"Yes."

"Is it a shotgun wedding? Do you need me to drive you crazy kids to Vegas? Ooh, can I be your bridesmaid? Should I book the Elvis chapel?"

Allison snorts. "It's a friendship ring, you boobsky."

"Wow! Still, pretty heavy stuff." I try to imagine Paul choosing a ring for Allison. I just can't. It's completely unimaginable. Maybe he let his mom choose it.

"Nah." Allison looks at the ring again and puts her mitten back on. "It's just a little token."

I'm oddly jealous and I have no idea why. I should be happy for her, but I feel kind of like you do when you give someone a sweater that you don't want anymore and they put it on and it somehow looks fabulous on them and you suddenly want it back even though you know it looks horrible on you.

With two levels and an escalator in the middle, the bookstore is enormous. It's the kind of place where you can go in looking for a book and come out with a yoga mat and a smoothie. Allison and I browse the magazines on the main floor to kill time. At two o'clock sharp we head up the escalator to the graphic novels. Paul is not there. We check Philosophy, World Religion, Sciences and even Self-Help, but Paul is not there either. Finally we spy him heading up the escalator with a tall, dark-haired boy and we hide among the mystery paperbacks. Paul heads toward the children's section and then does an about-face and comes our way. The dark-haired boy doesn't even notice Paul going off-course. I can't see them very well from our hiding spot, but they seem to be absorbed in animated conversation. I'm surprised Paul got here at all.

We watch them browse the graphic novels, and after a few moments, Allison and I pretend to talk to each other as we round the corner to where Paul and Joshua are standing.

"Let me just show you this one book I really love," says Allison.

Paul, hearing her voice, turns around. "Hey! Hi! I didn't know you were coming here today!"

Okay, so no Academy Award for Paul this year.

"Oh, and hi, Clare!" he adds. "What a nice surprise!"

Ugh, I could die. "Hi, Paul."

"Clare, Allison, this is my friend, Joshua, from school."

I smile my thin-lipped, nervous smile that I reserve for situations that are deeply uncomfortable. "Hi, Joshua."

Joshua is dressed for success. He looks like he could be my lawyer and I look like I could be his client who just got picked up for shoplifting. He's wearing a navy wool car coat with a crisp, pale blue Oxford shirt underneath and loafers (loafers!). He has tortoiseshell glasses on and he's very pale with black wavy hair. He also looks vaguely familiar but I don't know why. He shakes our hands, mine first and then Allison's, lawyer-style.

Joshua is a geek, there's no doubt about that, but as geeks go, he's not bad. He's the opposite of Vince, of course, the kind of guy who can disappear in a crowd, but he's quite tall and very thin. I suddenly wish I'd at least bothered to apply lip gloss. He's looking at me intently, as if he's trying to place me.

"I know you from somewhere."

"No, you don't." I blush and look away. I wish he would stop looking at me like I have food in my teeth (which is entirely possible).

"Yes, I do."

"You do?"

"Yes. Weren't you outside the tae kwon do studio last night with a dog?"

Suddenly it all comes clear. He's the guy with the black belt who was so impressive. The glasses threw me. He wasn't wearing them yesterday. Now I'm *really* wishing I wasn't dressed like a bag lady. I run my hand through my stringy hair. I try to remember if I washed it yesterday.

"That was you?" I ask. "You're really good."

Allison jumps in. "Wow, what a crazy coincidence! Clare was just talking about tae kwon do yesterday and then, *boom*! Here you are, tae kwon do guy! Isn't that a crazy coincidence, Clare?"

I raise my left eyebrow at her, which means, "Who *are* you?"

Paul jumps in as if he's reading from a script. "Hey, why don't we go to the café for a drink or something?"

"Sure," I say woodenly.

So off we go to the café, conveniently located next to the cookbooks. Allison and I grab a table while Joshua and Paul get the drinks.

"So, what do you think?" asks Allison before we even sit down.

"He seems nice. I feel horrible for treating him like he's a used car I'm thinking about buying. Let's just pretend this really was a coincidence from here on, okay?"

"Sure," Allison smiles. Her work is done.

I watch Joshua and Paul at the counter. You'd never guess that the rather stiff-looking, skinny guy standing with Paul could be capable of what I saw yesterday. It's a bit like meeting Clark Kent out of his Superman tights. Except Clark Kent never really looked like a geek, even in his glasses. I always thought Lois Lane was an idiot for not figuring out who he was immediately.

When they arrive with our drinks, Joshua puts my Coke in front of me and won't take any money for it, even when I insist. Paul won't take any money from Allison either, even though I know he would if Joshua hadn't set an example. Paul believes in splitting everything evenly. He used to do the math in his head when we were at the Dairy Delite and tell me to the penny what I owed.

Joshua asks polite questions about my life and school and I ask polite questions back. He has a thoughtful way of answering questions, pausing for so long before answering that you think he might not have heard you. When I ask him about tae kwon do his eyes change just a bit. His pupils get bigger behind his tortoiseshell frames and he leans in a little closer to me. Turns out he's been practising for eight years. (So much for a little distraction. This is a lifelong commitment.) He asks me why I was at the studio and I tell him I was thinking about taking lessons. This seems to excite him — as much as a guy like Joshua can get excited. He tells me that I should come by the *dojang* later and he'll introduce me to his instructor. I tell him I'd like that very much. Allison and Paul beam at us like proud parents.

When Joshua talks he moves his hands carefully; he looks down at them whenever he pauses. His fingers are long and thin like Vince's, but not as graceful. They're a bit knobby at the joints. I suddenly have a flashback of Vince kissing the girl with the braids who dresses a million times better than me. I imagine Vince holding hands with her and watching her with those pale blue eyes. Joshua's eyes are not soft like Vince's; they're intense and probing, but he has perfectly shaped eyebrows and ridiculously long lashes.

Eventually, talk gets around to what everyone's doing for New Year's. I casually mention to Joshua that I've invited Paul and Allison over and ask him if he'd like to join us. He says sure and asks what he should bring.

"A Jell-O mould would be nice," I say.

"Okay," he says, uncertainly.

"Kidding," I say.

"Oh." He blushes.

I smile at him, my real smile this time, and he smiles back.

Chapter 20

Yesterday I didn't know what a *dojang* was. Today I'm standing in one, wearing white pajamas (actually called a *dobok*) with a white belt (white on white? Elsa would be mortified). The white belt signifies innocence and no knowledge of tae kwon do yet. Yup, that's me. Joshua told me that I had to be on time and I couldn't wear any jewellery (I had to explain that I can't take the silver hoops out) or even chew gum. Plus — and this is a big one — you're not supposed to talk in the *dojang*. What have I gotten myself into here? Joshua is standing next to me in roughly the same outfit. He's just introduced me to his instructor, Koh Don Joo, who bowed slightly and I bowed back, which seemed like the right thing to do. Koh Don Joo is about a foot shorter than Joshua and he's way older than my dad, but something tells me that he could take him if he wanted to.

I'm here for a sort of introduction to tae kwon do. It's supposed to help you better understand what it's all about so you can decide if you'd like to proceed. I feel very silly doing all of this in front of someone I've only known for one day (technically, half a day). It feels like a crash course in "Getting to Know You."

Even though I'm allegedly here for the tae kwon do, I've washed and conditioned my hair and even applied a touch of mascara and some subtle pink lip gloss. I don't want Joshua to think I always look like a slob.

The instructor claps his hands and our ragtag group gathers obediently in front of him. There's only one other girl in the group, a small, thin, serious-looking Asian girl. Her brow is furrowed with concentration and she stares straight ahead. I'm about twice her size but I'm starting to understand that size means nothing in tae kwon do. Joshua disappears to the other side of the room to quietly practise his kicks.

Koh Don Joo explains to us the Tenets of Tae Kwon Do: Courtesy, Integrity, Perseverance, Self-Control and Indomitable Spirit. He tells us that the final goal of tae kwon do is to achieve harmony with nature and oneself. Balance is gained by controlling both evil and good forces, Yin versus Yang. A true tae kwon do student knows how to behave in all situations. It all sounds great but my head is spinning and I haven't even moved yet. This tae kwon do stuff is a lot more complicated than I thought. I kind of wish I'd gotten started earlier, like maybe when I was four.

Koh Don Joo teaches us some basic stances. He tells us the name of each one in English and then in Korean. Okay, no one told me I would have to learn a whole new language. We start with Parallel Stance, or *Naranhi Sohgi*. No problem. That one's a snap. Then we learn Ready Stance, or *Pyoni Sohgi*. Easy. Then there's Closed Feet Stance, or *Moa Sohgi*. Easy as pie. Walking Stance. Ditto. And finally, Forward Stance. I master the stances. I am the Queen of the Stances. I look over at Joshua to see if he was watching my impressive stances but he's busy kicking an imaginary opponent in the head.

Next, Koh Don Joo teaches us some blocking techniques, or *Maggi*. They're all pretty easy, but then again, we're blocking thin air. I assume that blocking a real opponent might be trickier. Things start to get a little more complicated when we move along to kicking techniques, or *Chagi*. I'm great at the Front Kick, but the Axe Kick gives me a lot of trouble, and forget about the Spinning Hook Kick. Koh Don Joo tells us not to worry if our kicks don't look great. It takes years of practice to perfect them. Years? Hmmm.

At the end of our introductory session Koh Don Joo bows again and we all bow back. He tells us that he hopes we all return next week to continue our studies. I'm going to have to give that some serious thought, but I have to admit I had a lot of fun. Plus, now I own my own *dobok*. I bought it at the Pro Shop of Inner Peace on the way in. Joshua comes over to see how it went and I tell him that I had a great time. He asks if he can walk me home, which is about the nicest thing a boy has ever asked me. I've heard about this whole "getting walked home" thing — I've even seen it on TV — but I like that I'm about to experience it first-hand. I know that I would never choose Joshua for a boyfriend but boys aren't exactly beating down my door and at least Joshua seems nice.

We walk out into the cold together wearing our *doboks* under our coats. We probably look like escapees from a mental institution. Joshua looks straight ahead. I study his profile. His nose is way too big for his face and as we walk I notice that it's turning red from the cold. He's wearing his glasses again and he looks very serious and very smart. I'm sort of expecting him to tell me all about the joys of tae kwon do but he doesn't even mention it. Maybe that's another rule, maybe you're not supposed to discuss it. I scramble for something to say as we walk but, unlike with Vince, I don't feel like I have to act cool or lie about anything. I finally think of something.

"So, are you eager to get back to school?"

He shrugs. "I like school but sometimes it feels so pointless. Just a way to get from A to B. I'm hoping to accelerate so that I can get done with high school early and get into pre-med."

"And then what?"

"I'm not sure. After medical school I think I'd like to work in epidemiology. Something like that."

"Wow. That's impressive. I can't even decide if I want to take track next year."

Joshua and I both have long legs. Usually, when I'm walking with someone, I feel like I'm walking way too fast for them, but Joshua and I walk perfectly in-step together. We come to a corner and he looks both ways before he steps off the curb, gently taking my elbow. I feel a bit like a princess.

"The big decisions are always easier for me," he continues. "It's the little stuff I can't make up my mind about.

You should see me order off a menu. My family has almost starved to death waiting for me."

"And do you do that thing where you open the refrigerator and stare at the food forever because you can't decide what you want to eat?"

"All the time. I also hold up the cafeteria line at school. No one wants to be behind me. And those fifty-flavour ice cream places? My head practically explodes."

We talk about my acting career, movies, music. (Oh, thank God! He likes normal music.) I'm getting used to Joshua's funny way of talking. He thinks hard about what he's going to say and he doesn't talk just for the sake of talking. When he does speak, it's slow and thoughtful. I decide that I like it. It makes me feel like he takes me seriously, like he's really listening to me.

As we turn onto my street, I see a hot pink snowsuit bobbing in the distance. But it's too late to hide: Patience has spied us. I quickly fill Joshua in on who she is as she heads toward us like a pink projectile.

"Do you guys want to make a snow fort?" she screams when she's still half a block away.

"Not right now, Patience. The snow's too melty."

"What?"

"THE SNOW'S TOO MELTY!" I yell back.

She stops in front of us and eyes Joshua suspiciously. "Are you the guy from the hospital?"

"No, Patience. That was Simon, this is Joshua."

"Are you Clare's boyfriend?" she asks.

Joshua considers the question. "No. I'm her friend," he says.

I pray that she doesn't continue with this line of questioning.

"*I'm* her friend! You can be her boyfriend. She doesn't have a boyfriend."

I shudder. "Thanks, Patience. We should get going now."

"Why are you dressed like doctors?" she asks, dragging her mitten across her nose.

"Because," I say, which seems to satisfy her.

"Wait! I have something to show you."

I sigh. She unzips the pocket on the front of her snowsuit and yanks off her striped wool mitten with her teeth. She digs around in the pocket and pulls out something tiny and white. She puts it in her open palm and presents it to us. It's a tooth. The gap in her smile clears up any mystery about where it came from.

"Look! It fell out when I was eating popcorn!"

Joshua pretends to admire it, which is awfully nice of him.

"The cookie monster is coming tonight to pay me for it," says Patience.

"The cookie monster? You mean the tooth fairy?" I ask.

"Right. That's what I meant. Well, I have to go to the bathroom now." She turns and tears up the street to her house, leaving us standing there.

"I'm up here on the right," I say. I decide to pretend that the last three minutes never happened. It isn't enough that Patience almost killed my dog. Now she mortifies me in front of a boy I barely know?

We cross the street and walk up the sidewalk to my house. I notice that both my parents' cars are in the driveway. Well, how could it be worse than what just happened?

"Would you like to come in for a minute?" I ask.

"Well, maybe just a minute."

I open the front door. Elsie attacks. Joshua holds his ground.

"Elsie, get down!" I command, as though she might listen.

"It's okay. I love dogs," says Joshua. He crouches down so he's eye level with her and gives her the kind of attention that only a dog-lover can give.

My parents arrive from opposite ends of the house. My mom's still doing that thing where she's relieved to see me alive and without a police escort. She looks at Joshua with delight. I think he must have "future doctor" written all over him. I introduce him and he shakes their hands politely. My mom invites him to dinner, which seems a bit premature to me, but he says he has to get home. He tells me that he'll talk to me soon and he leaves. I close the door behind him and lean against it. My parents stand there beaming at me.

"I don't suppose you'd believe me if I told you he was wanted for armed robbery."

Chapter 21

I dab concealer on a mountainous pimple that's emerged on my chin overnight. As I study my face in the mirror, I think about how, only a couple of weeks ago, I'd secretly imagined myself getting ready for New Year's Eve just like I am now, except the person ringing my doorbell at eight wouldn't be Joshua, but Vince. I would float down the stairs wearing something fabulous and swing open the door and he'd be standing there, in a suit, flashing his amazing crooked-toothed smile.

Life is funny that way. Here I am, getting ready to spend New Year's Eve with an entirely different guy. And when I say different, I mean about as different as you can get. I remind myself to focus on the "New Year's with a guy" part because the alternative is New Year's alone feeling sorry for myself.

I'm resurrecting the black scoop-necked T-shirt and the Italian jeans Aunt Rusty gave me. I found them in a heap at the bottom of my closet where they've been since I flung them there the night of the party. I apply a little pale pink gloss to my lips and a bit of pink blush to my cheekbones. In my mirror, I see Elsa appear behind me. She's sprawled across my bed in a black cocktail dress and black stilettos. The long string of pearls around her neck forms a puddle on the bed. She rests her chin on her open palm and watches me.

"Is that what you're wearing?" she asks, with disapproval in her voice.

"I thought I might. It's not a party. It's just friends stopping by."

Elsa glances at her painted fingernails. "Really? Just friends?"

I turn around to face her. "Are you kidding me? I just met him and besides, I'm still recovering from ... well, you know."

Elsa plays with her pearls. "Ah yes, the bad boy. Are we still smarting from that?"

"A little. Okay, a lot."

"This Joshua guy. He's awfully nice."

"Yes. He's nice."

"Let's not knock nice."

"I'm not. I'm just taking my time getting to know him."

"Fair enough, but don't take *too* long. He's leaving soon."

"Don't rush me."

"Who's rushing?"

"So, how do I look?"

Elsa gives me the once-over. "Well, considering you're not really going anywhere, I think you look great, but it's a little casual for my taste."

"Yeah, well, if it were up to you, I'd wear a cocktail dress to the grocery store."

"Hey, wait a second. What are those things in your ears?"

"I thought you'd never notice. I had them done the other day at the mall."

"Fabulous. I mean those hoops are a little puny but they're just for now, right?"

"I happen to like these hoops, but yes, in six weeks I can take them out and wear anything." Elsa is wearing pearls in her ears.

"What fun!" She looks me over again. "Aren't you forgetting something?"

"What?"

"A woman should always wear a touch of unforgettable fragrance. Parisian women are naked without it."

I pull open my underwear drawer and dig around for the tiny bottle of French violet perfume that magically appeared on my bed the morning of my thirteenth birthday.

"Just a touch," says Elsa. "You want him to remember you, not be repelled by you."

I dab a bit on my wrists and behind my earlobes. I carefully replace the lid and put the bottle back in my drawer.

"Well, I should get downstairs. Where are you spending New Year's?"

"Darling, New Year's is over in Paris. Remember? We're eight hours ahead of you."

"Right. How was it?"

Elsa flips over onto her back. "It had its moments but mostly I was bored as a brick."

I sit down in my rocker, across from her. "Are you tired of Paris?"

Elsa sits up, looking serious. "Are you?" she asks.

"I don't know."

"You're not going to banish me to some sort of retirement home for imaginary friends who've outlived their usefulness, are you?"

I can't bear to look her in the eye. She looks devastated.

"Of course not. Don't be stupid." I stand up and look in the mirror once more. Behind me the bed is empty.

Downstairs, my parents are on their way out to a fancy party. My mom looks stunning in a green cocktail dress and my dad is wearing a tuxedo that looks a wee bit tight.

"Dad, you look great," I say, as I pass him in the hallway.

"You think so? I haven't worn this thing for a year and I think the cleaners must have shrunk it or something."

My mom winks at me as she comes over to tie his bow tie. "Just don't eat and you'll be fine."

The doorbell rings. I grab Elsie by the collar and open the door. Paul and Joshua and Allison are standing there, smiling. Paul and Joshua are wearing their matching navy overcoats with navy V-neck sweaters underneath. A school crest is embroidered on the right side of their chests. Crisp white collars and cuffs poke out from their sweaters. They couldn't look more Private Boys' School. The effect is quite handsome though, especially in Joshua's case. I wonder if it's too late to run upstairs and change into a cocktail dress, and then I remember that I don't own any. Besides, a girl really shouldn't be wearing a cocktail dress until she's old enough to drink one. Thankfully, Allison is wearing a sloppier version of what I have on. She holds up a DVD of *Manhattan*, my favourite Woody Allen movie.

"Three video stores, but I got it," she says.

I invite them in and take their coats as they exchange polite "hellos" with my parents. My dad is so thrilled with Joshua that if we lived in another country, I'm sure he'd be negotiating a promise of marriage by throwing in a few goats or something. My mom has to pry him away from us. He seems like he'd rather stay home with us and engage Joshua in a man-to-man about his promising future as a breadwinner.

My parents finally leave and we move into the living room. This is, thankfully, the last night of our winter wonderland. The pine boughs are starting to gather dust and the Christmas tree is looking dry and sad. Tomorrow morning, my mom will tear down the Christmas decorations in a fevered flurry before my dad and I even open our eyes. The only thing she'll leave is the giant tree stripped of its decorations for my dad to somehow wrestle out into the yard. There's enough wood on that thing to build a log cabin but I'm pretty sure that won't occur to him.

Allison helps herself to our CD collection and puts on one of my mom's Bob Dylan CDs. I get the phone and we order two pizzas, one vegetarian and one with pepperoni.

Allison sits next to Paul on the sofa and makes fascinating small talk while I sit stiffly across from Joshua in an armchair with absolutely nothing to say. Allison tries her best to draw me into the conversation but I can only provide my thin, uncomfortable smile. I seem to have forgotten how to converse. I realize that this can only mean one thing: I must like Joshua more than I'm admitting even to myself.

Just as I'm thinking that my New Year's is going to be a complete disaster, something wonderful happens.

Chapter 22

Joshua notices it first. He stands up and walks over to the window.

"Wow. Look at that. It's snowing."

We all get up, stand next to him at the window and watch the soft fluffy flakes float past. It hasn't snowed since the night I walked to Simon's play with Paul and Allison. All the pretty white snow has disappeared since then, leaving ugly brown slush and grey snowbanks. We watch the snow fall in silence as though we're sharing some sort of religious experience. Suddenly Allison makes a beeline for the front door.

"Last one outside's a rotten egg!" she calls over her shoulder.

We follow her and race to pull on our boots and coats. Paul starts to protest, mentioning something about his school clothes, but we all ignore him so he reluctantly pulls his coat on.

As I'm leaning over to pull on a boot, Allison whispers in my ear, "Snap out of it! You're on a date!"

We stand on the sidewalk in front of my house, looking up at the flakes. It's strangely quiet on my street. The only sound is the buzz of the streetlights. Allison disappears behind us and suddenly a wet, cold snowball explodes on my shoulder. War has been declared.

Joshua and I team up and start pelting snowballs at Allison and Paul. Allison is a great shot and nails Joshua in the back as we dive behind a shrub and load up with ammunition. Paul is a sitting duck and I get him in the chest.

"Hey, watch the glasses!" he yells, as another snowball hits him in the thigh. Allison pulls him behind an icy snowbank.

We continue firing at each other. Allison is brave and comes out from behind the snowbank to take aim, but Paul stays where it's safe. Joshua is a better shot than I am but I make a great snowball so I feed him ammo. Elsie runs from one team to the other, trying to catch the snowballs in her mouth. After several minutes of uninterrupted fire, a car with a light on top of it pulls up in front of the house. At first I think it's the cops, here to respond to a call about a disturbance, but it's the pizza guy so we call a truce. I run inside for the money my mom left me to pay him. Everyone else staggers in and we pull off our wet coats.

We all sit in front of the fireplace with rosy cheeks and wolf down the pizza. Allison puts on the *Beach Boys' Greatest Hits*, which may seem wildly inappropriate for a winter's night but somehow surf music couldn't be more perfect. We talk non-stop and laugh a lot. I tease Paul the way I used to before he left for school and Joshua joins in with a ton of stories from school that I've never heard before. Paul has a new confidence, though. I'm pretty sure it's because of Allison. Even though I don't understand the attraction, I guess I'm glad that my two friends found each other.

I sit close to Joshua on the floor, our legs almost touching but not quite. The more I look at him, the more I see. He has a funny laugh, and he never laughs unless he means it. Everything about Joshua is so real. He never tries to be something he's not. I really like that. We put the movie on and stack up the pillows on the floor in front of the television. Allison arranges herself right next to Paul and I get comfortable between Paul and Joshua. Elsie lies sleeping at our feet. We watch the movie without talking. Allison and I never talk during Woody Allen movies. I'm glad we don't have to tell anyone that. I've seen this movie three times and Allison's seen it twice. I know a lot of it by heart. The movie ends at 11:55 p.m. I stretch and look over at Paul and Allison. They're asleep. I nudge Joshua and point at them. He smiles.

I find the remote and click to a TV station that's showing the countdown in Times Square and we watch the New Year approach. As the ball drops at the stroke of midnight, Joshua turns to me and it looks like he's about to kiss me. I'm all ready, except that out of the blue, I start to hiccup. Not ladylike little hiccups that you can hide, but big body-shaking ones. Joshua starts to laugh and I do, too, so now I'm giggling between hiccups. Joshua hands me his soda. I take a few sips and stop hiccupping and laughing just long enough for him to squeeze in a kiss. Probably not the kiss he was imagining, not the most romantic kiss ever, but he kisses me in a way that's completely different from when Vince kissed me, or even when Simon kissed me. He kisses me like he means it, but it's so soft that I can barely feel it. At that moment I'm sure that this is our first of many kisses. That's what Joshua does: he makes you feel sure of yourself.

When he pulls away from me he says, "Happy New Year" and I smile at him and say the same. His hand lingers on my upper arm for a moment. It feels soft and cool. I'm so happy that I spent my New Year's Eve getting to know him better. My hiccups come back full-strength.

After a while we wake up Paul and Allison, who can't believe that we let them sleep through New Year's. Allison is furious and I know it's mostly because she missed anything that might have happened between Joshua and me. She and Paul kiss half-heartedly, still sleepy and yawning. It's hard to watch Paul kiss Allison because in a million years I could never have imagined Paul kissing anyone, let alone my best friend. I'm glad I don't barf. We clean up the empty pizza boxes and put the cushions back on the sofa. My friends put on their wet coats and boots and we say goodbye. Joshua says he'll call me and I know that he will. I lock the door behind them. My parents will probably be home soon, carrying noisemakers and talking loudly. I unplug the Christmas tree for the last time and make my way upstairs. Elsie jumps on my bed and curls up with a deep sigh.

I take off my clothes and start to put on my Spider-Man pajamas, but something makes me choose a soft pink nightie instead. I pull it over my head and look at myself in the mirror. I like the way I look. I turn on my reading lamp and get into bed.

Dear Elsa,

So, you were right. Joshua became more than a friend tonight. I think I may have finally done something right in the boy department. On Sunday he'll be gone and on Monday I'll be back at school. Auditions for The Taming of the Shrew are coming up in two weeks and I'm auditioning for the part of Katharina, so I'll have to start learning my lines. On Tuesday, I start tae kwon do classes at the dojang. I can't imagine what I'm in for but I'm sure it will be an adventure.

Who could have guessed that Christmas vacation would be such a life-changing experience for me? I would have been happy with presents and chocolate. I wanted to tell you that I'm glad you showed up to help me figure things out. It's a fresh new year and I'm supposed to make a resolution but I can't think of anything I want to change about my life right now, especially not you. And just for the record, Ms. Ganz is still wrong about everything.

Happy New Year,

Clare

Chapter 23

Dear Clare,

Thanks for the postcard. I love the old picture of Godzilla on the front. I've tacked it to the bulletin board above the desk where I study (which I'm supposed to be doing right now) so I can think of you whenever I sit here. Not that I'm not thinking of you anyway. I feel really cheated that I only got to see you a few times before I left for school, but I'm really glad you came over to my house to see me off, even though it was 6:00 a.m. and you looked like you could have used a lot more sleep. I kind of like the way you look all rumpled and sleepy though.

Congratulations on landing the part of Katharina! I knew you were perfect for it. We studied *The Taming of the Shrew* last year in English so I know the part well. It's a great role for you. I should be home in time for opening night. Luckily, it coincides with my spring break. No doubt you'll be consumed with rehearsals for the next little while. I hope you don't wear yourself out.

Classes here are really intense and we don't get left with a lot of free time. I'm back swimming every morning before class but it's just to clear my head a bit. I'm not swim team material or anything like that. My roommate, Darwin, is on the team and he swims about three times faster than I do. It's pretty embarrassing when he gets several laps ahead of me. He's really nice about it though. He never laughs at me. Mostly because I lend him all my class notes. He looks like a Greek god but he's an awful student. He has two girlfriends on separate sides of the country. They both look like supermodels.

I still practise my tae kwon do every day. Actually, there's a small group of us here who practise together. I'm really glad that you're enjoying your classes, too. It's a great discipline once you get the hang of it. The more you do it, the more it creeps into other parts of your life, and before you know it, you're looking at everything a little differently. I think you'll make an excellent student and I'm sure that Koh Don Joo is taking good care of you.

Paul is desperately missing Allison and he talks about her non-stop. I guess you know that your friend has completely changed his life. He never dreamed he could find a girlfriend like Allison — or any girlfriend at all for that matter. I've never seen him so happy. She's awfully special and, let's face it, if it weren't for her twisting your arm, we never would have met.

I think about New Year's Eve a lot; sometimes our short time alone is all I think about. It helps get me through some awfully boring classes. I hope we can pick up where we left off when I get home, even though you'll be busy with the play. I'd like to get to know you a lot better. I gathered from your postcard that you feel the same way.

Our phone calls are restricted here (not unlike a penitentiary). We're only allowed to use cell phones for emergencies and on the weekends, so I will try to call you this weekend.

XOXO,

Joshua

P.S. Can you send me a photo of yourself? It will help me get through the rest of the winter.

I fold the letter and slip it back into its envelope. I've read it so many times that it slides in effortlessly. I turn it over and look at the front of the envelope, running my finger over my name written in Joshua's tidy handwriting. I look at the return address again, so far away from me.

At first I wondered why he didn't just e-mail me but now that I'm holding his letter in my hand, I understand perfectly. A real letter is a keepsake.

Strange buildings and neighbourhoods whiz past the big bus windows. I'm on my way to the first rehearsal for *The Taming of the Shrew*. It's being staged by a youth theatre group downtown called Three Toads in a Small Box. Eric told me about it and he encouraged me to audition. He even came to the audition. I was up against seven other girls for the part of Katharina and I got it! I'm so nervous I can barely breathe. My mom wanted to drive me today but I insisted on taking the bus. I figure that when you do something new, every single bit of it should be new. I touch the new gold hoops in my ears, my mom's contribution to my new part. She told me that they look very dramatic. She also told me she'd kill me if I lost them.

I watch the scenery out the window for a moment and then I take out my pen and turn to an empty page in my notebook.

Dear Joshua . . .

For everyone's information, running bras are kept in the lingerie department and not the sporting goods department as I had hoped. Needless to say, buying a running bra turned out to be a lot more traumatic than I thought it would be.

My mom and I found the lingerie department tucked away in a corner all on its own, and it was, in a word, pink. Pink everywhere you looked: walls, carpet, even the fitting rooms. A saleslady wearing pink floated over to us, smiling as though she were welcoming us into her own home.

"Good morning!" she said, clasping her hands together in front of her. "How can I help you today?" She flashed us a set of enormous teeth with fuchsia lipstick all over them. The better to eat me with, I'm sure. I contemplated making a run for it.

My mother took charge. She's always had a "take-no-prisoners" approach to shopping. "We're looking for running bras for my daughter," she announced.

"I see," said the saleslady, looking at my chest, or rather, looking *for* my chest. I swallowed hard.

"Have you ever been fitted for a bra, dear?" she asked me.

I opened my mouth but nothing came out. Finally I squeaked, "No."

My mother came to my rescue again. "I don't think that's necessary for a running bra, do you?"

I silently thanked her.

The pink saleslady seemed a little miffed. Measuring my measly chest seemed to be something she would have enjoyed immensely. It made me wonder what her days were like.

"All right then," she said curtly, "this way please." She ushered us to the proper section. She said, "Athletic bras come in extra-small, small, medium, large and extra large. We carry a wide variety of styles and colours." She showed us a blur of bras. She was well-versed in all aspects of the "athletic bra" but, looking at her, I had my doubts she'd ever worn one. One thing I knew for certain: this woman was born to sell lingerie.

Thankfully there was no one else in the department except a girl about my age and her mother. They appeared to be going through virtually the same process as we were and the girl looked as horrified as I felt. She caught my eye and made a face. We both laughed. She had long brown hair pulled into a ponytail, and she was wearing jeans with a tear in the knee exactly where my favourite jeans were torn. My mom wouldn't let me wear mine to the mall, though. I wanted to point out to her that these perfectly decent-looking people had no problem with torn jeans. The girl also had a fake tattoo of a butterfly on her right arm and she was chewing bright-green gum. I wondered why I'd never seen her before.

My mom chose about a hundred bras for me to try on and followed the saleslady to the pink fitting rooms. I reluctantly trailed behind. Soft music played as the lady unlocked the fitting room with a key from around her wrist. I personally questioned the need for high security. Why would anyone want to break into these stupid pink cubicles? Out, sure, but in?

My mom stood guard outside my fitting room as I danced in the mirror to a cheesy instrumental version of U2's "I Still Haven't Found What I'm Looking For" and tried on about half the bras she'd picked out. The other half were out of the question. I heard the girl with the brown ponytail talking to her mom about the bras she was trying on a few doors down. She was using words like "hideous" and "grotesque." It was kind of comforting.

My mom and I finally settled on two bras: a black one that I picked out and a flesh-toned one that my mom insisted on. Just whose flesh do they base the colour "flesh-tone" on, anyway? Certainly not mine. It reminded me of an Ace bandage, but my mom wasn't taking no for an answer, so I went along with it because she was such a good sport about the black one. The pink saleslady wrapped my bras in lots of pink tissue and put them in a shiny pink bag, which is the equivalent of carrying a neon sign that says, "I've been to the lingerie department!" She flashed her pink teeth at us one more time and wished us a pleasant day.

We headed out into the mall to the sporting goods store. After the bra-buying experience, buying sneakers was going to be a breeze. I was back in familiar territory. And I was right: my feet had grown another size. Maybe it was a fair trade-off for my new chest but I was ready for them to stop growing any time. I chose a pair of running shoes that were so comfortable I was pretty sure I could leap tall buildings in a single bound. I asked the gangly, pimply sales clerk in the referee's uniform for an extra-large bag so I could hide the pink lingerie bag inside it.

With both missions accomplished we headed back to the parking garage and searched for the car. In all the years we've been going places together, my mother and I have never once taken note of where the car is parked. Each level of the parking garage was conveniently named after a type of tree: Fir, Pine, Oak — basically the names of trees they cut down to build the mall. They all sounded the same to us. It would be so much easier if they named the levels after animals: Penguin, Grizzly Bear, Python. That I would remember. We finally found the car on Spruce, hiding between two suvs.

When we got home, I took the bags up to my room and unpacked the bras. I put the flesh-toned one in my drawer with my socks and I put the black one on. I posed in front of the mirror in it and tried it on with almost every piece of clothing in my closet, as though I would be wearing only the bra and nothing over it. I practised talking to Mr. Bianchini in my new bra for a while, then I took a pair of sweat socks and put one in each cup to get an idea of what I might look like down the road. I looked absurd. My mom came upstairs to tell me to wash the bras before I wore them. She walked in when I was one sock out and one sock in. At first she looked alarmed, but when she realized it was just a sock, she laughed.

"I actually went to school like that once," she said.

I tried to imagine my mom at my age, going to school with socks in her bra, but all I could picture was a girl in a little navy suit, carrying a briefcase, handing out business cards over lunch. It was impossible to imagine my mom ever being as lost as I feel sometimes ...

Still There, Clare

978-1-55192-828-9
$10.95 CDN / $9.95 US

Ask your bookseller about
Still There, Clare
and other great titles
from Raincoast Books!

THE CLARE SERIES IS ANCIENT-FOREST FRIENDLY

By printing *Double-Dare Clare* on paper made from 100% recycled fibre rather than virgin tree fibre, Raincoast Books has made the following ecological savings:

- 21 trees
- 2,011 kilograms of carbon dioxide (equivalent to driving an average North American car for about five months)
- 17 million BTUs (equivalent to the power consumption of a North American home for over two months)
- 12,322 litres of water
- 753 kilograms of solid waste diverted from landfill

Environmental savings were estimated by Markets Initiative using the Environmental Defense Paper Calculator. For more information, visit www.papercalculator.org.

RAINCOAST BOOKS
www.raincoast.com

ANCIENT FOREST
FRIENDLY

PHOTO: ALEX GREEN

About the Author

Yvonne Prinz was born and raised in Edmonton, Alberta. *Double-Dare Clare* is her third novel in a series of books about the quirky and loveable Clare and her savvy alter ego, Elsa. Book One in the series, *Still There, Clare*, was first published by Raincoast Books in 2004. Yvonne lives in the San Francisco Bay area, where she and her husband founded a chain of independent record stores.

www.stillthereclare.com